"All right, hold it!!
leaped in front of the open car.

Josh stood at the edge of the doorway holding a box of Swiss watches in front of him. His eyes bulged at the sight of the white man with the gun pointed at his head.

"You fuckin' littl' nigger boy!" Wilbur felt his hand begin to tremble. "Get down off there, black boy!"

Josh stared down the barrel of the gun, opened his mouth and tried to speak. But nothing came out. Suddenly he fell to his knees. He began to cry—hysterical sobs of panic that sounded more like laughter than pain.

The shot was fired directly into Josh's tear-stained cheek, tearing away the entire left side of his skull. The second shot entered his neck and ripped the muscles and cords out of his body. As his skinny little body flew backward into the dark recesses of the boxcar, Josh's skull and throat were splattered against the boxes of imported watches.

Suddenly Buddy turned and ran back into the boxcar jungle. Wilbur stood with his back toward the approaching youth. At that moment Buddy was arcing his nunchaku toward the white man's skull. Wilbur did not even have time to register the shrill, eerie scream before the hard wood struck him.

Holloway House Originals by Donald Goines

DOPEFIEND
WHORESON
BLACK GANGSTER
STREET PLAYERS
WHITE MAN'S JUSTICE,
   BLACK MAN'S GRIEF
BLACK GIRL LOST
CRIME PARTNERS
CRY REVENGE
DADDY COOL
DEATH LIST
ELDORADO RED
INNER CITY HOODLUM
KENYATTA'S ESCAPE
KENYATTA'S LAST HIT
NEVER DIE ALONE
SWAMP MAN

Special Preview of *Eldorado Red*—page 223

INNER CITY HOODLUM

Donald Goines

www.kensingtonbooks.com

DONALD GOINES' completed manuscript of *Inner City Hoodlum* was discovered shortly after his tragic and violent death, making it the last known work by this talented black author. Had Donald lived to see his book reach publication he would have, as before, dedicated it to family, friends, and associates. But the bullets of an unknown killer cut Donald down. Therefore we take the opportunity to dedicate this final reflection of Donald's life to him and his efforts to express the rage, frustration and torment of a black man in America.

—The Publishers

JOHNNY WASHINGTON drove his old Chevy up the steep bank of the Fourth Street exit, turned left and moved down into the deserted, cavernous canyons of downtown Los Angeles. The streets were empty and dark. Everyone had fled the urban center the moment their working day had ended. Very few would dare to stay in the downtown district after dark.

"It's like the whole fuckin' place is ours for the askin'!" Buddy laughed. His large belly shook and his deep black face glistened. Most people looking at Buddy for the first time would have written him off as a teenage fatty, one of those kids who everyone would pick on. But those who knew him better and were able to detect the fact that he carried nunchaku sticks beneath his shirt knew a whole lot better. Johnny Washington knew Buddy's strength and Buddy's desire to inflict harm with that club, and that's why he had him with him every time he went on a job.

"Listen, my man," Johnny replied, turning his gaunt, black face toward Buddy, "this here shit downtown's for the fucking winos, man. We got better shit to hit at the yards." Johnny Washington was tall and lean, and he sat higher than either Buddy or Josh, who was in the backseat. Naturally when the man driving spoke both young men in the car listened.

"Someday? Huh, Johnny, someday?" Josh spoke in a nervous stutter. He was sixteen years old, the youngest of the trio by a year. Short and thin, his future was written in dark, black etchings across his worried face. The streets of Watts had gotten to Josh a long time ago, and no matter how hard he tried to fight back they were taking their toll.

"Yeah, Josh. Someday us three'll be sitting just a little higher. We can't miss. We got the brains, the brawn and the worried man. Now, how could a trio like ours ever blow it?" Johnny spoke through clenched teeth, his cigarette bobbing wildly as he spoke.

"We goin' take this whole fuckin' jiveass town by the fuckin' throat and make it ours! Ain' no doubt in my mind 'bout that, Johnny! No doubt!"

Johnny glanced across at his young companion, remembering the days when the neighborhood kids had picked on the poor little fat boy and ridiculed him in public. Buddy had had nowhere to turn until Johnny came along and taught him all he knew about street fighting, and especially about the use of the deadly nunchaku. Two long wooden sticks, the nunchaku if handled properly could penetrate a man's skull in one swift motion. Buddy had learned to use the instrument of death too well. The first time his neighborhood bully had tried to ridicule him, Buddy had violently cracked the six-footer's shoulder blade. The dead silence that followed the surprise beating indicated to everyone that Buddy was not to be teased any more. Johnny Washington had taught the teenager how to earn his self-respect, and Buddy would never forget. Buddy would always be Johnny's man, a loyal and devoted subject to whatever cause Johnny served.

As Johnny thought about Buddy, he noticed a squad car cruising slowly north on Main Street. Quickly, he turned south and passed the two policemen casually. He saw their white, suspicious faces peering at him from the interior of the black and white. He wasn't worried because he knew that, if you gave them the least amount of accessibility, they wouldn't bother you. No cops wanted to stop a group of blacks in the middle of a deserted city late at night for no good reason.

"Motherfuckers!" Buddy cursed under his breath, gripping his sticks tightly.

"Hey, Johnny, they're slowing down, man!" Josh was turned around and peering out the back window.

"Josh, baby," Johnny began, starting to laugh, "if I

had your fucking nerves I would have been fried out by this time! Man, you just got to learn to be cool. Okay?"

"Hey, they made a right turn! Beautiful!" Josh slumped down in his seat, pulled out a pack of Pall Malls and passed the cigarettes around. "Fuckin' way to make a livin'!"

Johnny laughed. "It ain't so bad, man. We just work our way through school, then become astronauts, you dig? We could make a fuckin' mint on those moon rocks...."

The three young men broke up laughing as Johnny turned onto Eighth Street and headed toward Santa Fe Avenue. The downtown district changed immediately from glass enclosed skyscrapers into dingy, decaying hotels and warehouses. Here a few late-night winos staggered along the filthy streets, trying to find their way home. Home to them was normally nothing more than a flea-bitten sleeping bag and cot, the smell of piss and the liquid in the next bottle. Johnny Washington looked at the remnants of what once were men and felt his stomach begin to churn. He thought of his father, sitting at home broke and jobless, and felt the anger boiling in his blood. Suddenly the joking and laughter had fled. Now it was down to the business at hand.

"Josh," Johnny began in a voice that was cold and direct, "you saw how many trains pull into the east side yard this morning?"

"Three. All of 'em from the harbor, too."

"That means we'll have the good shit at the south

end. The fuckin' guard won't even know we've been there till morning."

"Yeah," Buddy replied. "No sweat, my man. No sweat."

They rode in silence along the darkened freight yards of the city of Los Angeles. The huge boxcars waited in silence until they could be pulled up alongside the loading docks and emptied. In them were every variation of consumer goods known to society. Televisions, radios, watches, clothing, calculators, food, cameras..., goods that none of the three young black men's families would ever be able to afford. These were prizes given to the white man for services rendered. Rewards, Johnny thought as he crossed the multiple series of tracks toward the east side, for being white.

Wilbur Mann watched the little television screen go blank. He stared at the test pattern for a moment, then angrily shut the thing off. No more television that night and that meant the little guard shack at the northeast end of the yards would be closing in on the white man until dawn.

"Fucking shit!" Wilbur said aloud, then lifted his large, flabby frame off the stool, ran his hand across his balding head and hitched up his pants. He glanced at the photograph of the naked blonde sprawled spread-eagle on a tiger rug and his mind drifted back to the afternoon when his bitch of a wife had laughed at him.

Wilbur had wanted his heavyset wife to go down

on him, like he had seen the woman doing in the book that Alonzo, the swing-shift guard, had brought to work. The photograph showed a huge black man standing above a young blonde white woman. Both men had teased each other about the size of the black man's cock, but neither had taken their eyes off the picture.

After a sleepless night, churning thoughts of blow jobs and the photograph burning through his brain, Wilbur had awakened with the urge. It had been late afternoon, and his wife had been sitting in front of their new color television set, eating her second bag of potato chips. Wilbur had walked up to her and pulled her against the bulge in his bathrobe.

She had screamed, then had laughed, telling him how ridiculous he looked. She had thought it was all too funny, then had turned back to her chips and her soap opera. Wilbur then went into the bathroom with his girlie magazine and satisfied himself.

Now, as the dark hours of the morning surrounded the little shack, Wilbur cursed. He cursed his wife, he cursed his job and he cursed himself. The paunchy white man was still cursing and mumbling to himself as he pulled on his jacket with the gold security badge and released the catch and checked to make sure there were six cartridges in the barrel of his .38 police special. The feel of the cold steel, the heavy weight of the gun—its very presence—brought him relief. He held the gun in both hands and fondled it, stroking the barrel slowly and lovingly. "Fuck that bitch," Wilbur exclaimed softly. "I got everything I need!"

With that, Wilbur stepped out into the damp Los Angeles morning. He pulled out a Camel and lit it, inhaled deeply, patted his gun and started walking slowly toward the south end of the yard.

Johnny cut the lights as he pulled up between two diesel transports and stopped. The fence loomed ten feet high in front of them, with two feet of barbed wire on top of that.

"Get the trunk, Josh."

Johnny lit a cigarette and waited as Josh scrambled out of the car, opened the trunk and ran toward the fence. The small black teenager held a large, woolen blanket and tossed it across the barbed wire. He then pulled both ends of the blanket down and tied a huge knot to secure it.

"Okay, Buddy, my man. Let's move!"

Buddy and Johnny climbed out of the car and each cupped his hand for Josh. In one lunge, Josh was rolling across the top of the fence and leaping down to the other side. Buddy followed next, then Johnny.

The jungle of boxcars would have presented a problem to anyone unfamiliar with the trains. But Johnny had been looting for three years already and he knew which carriers to hit. The Southern Pacific lines were always the best. Coming out of Long Beach and down from San Francisco they carried imported goods. The watches, radios and cameras were the easiest to handle and brought the most money.

Johnny moved briskly between the boxcars, going more on instinct than anything else until he came to a Southern Pacific car that looked good. The door was facing them, away from the city side of the yard. The car was solid, not a refrigerator and not slatted for livestock.

"This is our baby, men," Johnny said.

"Let's get the fucker...." Buddy whispered as he held his nunchaku between the bolt latch and the frame of the door.

Johnny watched his chubby black friend with amazement. It always astounded him to see Buddy transform into a silent and muscular bull when there was work to be done. The muscles in Buddy's shoulders seemed to emerge magically from beneath his layers of fat. His entire body seemed to solidify into one massive power.

Buddy held each end of his sticks, took a deep and silent breath, then yelled out in a high-pitched scream as he drove all of his energy and concentration into the club. With a solid snap the huge bolt-lock spun off the frame and fell to the dirt.

"You are somethin' else, Buddy," Johnny whispered softly.

"It's nothin'. Just knowin' where to put it at the right time. No sweat." Buddy grinned broadly, his white teeth sparkling against his black skin.

Josh was already up into the car, searching with his flashlight. Buddy and Johnny waited below.

"Hey babies! It's a motherfuckin' gold mine! Watches! Man, this place is crawling with watches!" Josh brought one carton containing a hundred Swiss watches to the edge of the car and proudly showed them to his friends.

"Motherfuck, Sam'll give us a goddamn hundred and fifty for each box!"

"Let's get it on!" Johnny knew what the risks were and knew that they didn't have too much time until the security guard made his hourly pass. If he spotted the Chevy parked between the trucks, he would investigate. They had twenty minutes left to get the boxes out of the car and over the fence.

The three worked silently and with teamwork. Josh piled three boxes into his partners' outstretched arms. Each man ran the boxes to the base of the fence and returned for another load. Johnny figured that they would have enough room in the car for twenty boxes.

Alone in the dark jungle of the boxcars, Wilbur Mann felt like a hunter. The strength that had been sapped from his body by too much booze and too much food seemed to return with each step he took. If only that chick in the photograph could see him now, he thought to himself. She would go down on me right away....

But then Wilbur's heart froze. In a flash, he saw two shadowy figures run between the space of the boxcars and disappear. Looters! Nine months ago Wilbur had confronted looters but they had escaped. He had spent the rest of the night trying to replace the boxes and fix the door to make it look as though nothing had ever happened. But not this time, the paunchy guard thought to himself. That shit's all over with.

The hunter returned, holding his .38 and moving quietly between the cars. He crept up to the side of the boxcar where Josh was and waited. He heard the noises of Josh moving the boxes around inside the boxcar. Wilbur cocked his pistol and moved along the edge of the car to the doorway.

"All right, hold it!!!" Wilbur screamed as he leaped in front of the open car.

Josh stood at the edge of the doorway holding a box of Swiss watches in front of him. His eyes bulged at the sight of the white man with the gun pointed at his head.

"You fuckin' littl' nigger boy!" Wilbur felt his hand begin to tremble. He brought up his other hand to steady his grip. "Get down off of there, black boy!"

"Don't shoot, mister! Please, don't shoot!" Josh was shaking wildly. His body was paralyzed with fear as he tried to obey the man's order. But he couldn't move. His nerves had gripped him as tightly as if he were caught in a winch.

"I said," Wilbur continued, feeling his words strongly and gaining confidence at the sight of the trembling youth, "for you to get your fuckin' black ass out of there!"

Josh stared down the barrel of the gun, opened his mouth and tried to speak. But nothing came out. Suddenly, he fell to his knees. He began to cry—hysterical sobs of panic that sounded more like laughter than pain.

Laughter was what Wilbur heard, also. His head began to spin, and he felt the first rush of madness shoot through his body like adrenalin.

The shot was fired directly into Josh's tear-stained cheek, tearing away the entire left side of his skull. The second shot entered his neck and ripped the muscles and cords out of his body. As his skinny little body flew backward into the dark recesses of the boxcar, Josh's skull and throat were being splattered against the boxes of imported watches.

Buddy and Johnny were standing on opposite sides of the fence when they heard the shots. For a moment neither man knew what to do. Suddenly Buddy turned and ran back into the boxcar jungle. Johnny climbed the fence a moment later and dropped to the other side.

Wilbur stood with his back toward the approaching youth. He held the pistol in both hands and still pointed it at the dismembered body of the black youth inside the boxcar.

Buddy pulled up behind the white man and stopped short. All he could see was the blood and pieces of skull inside the car.

The little guard was at that moment seething with a kind of angry joy at what he had done. For those brief moments, he had come to be the man once again. The kid inside the boxcar was dead, and he, Wilbur Mann, had killed him. The kid was a nigger and that had made it even better. Wilbur felt something at that moment that he had not felt in a long time. He wanted a woman.

The image of the naked woman on his little shack wall was the last thing that Wilbur Mann would ever see. At that moment Buddy was arcing his nunchaku toward the white man's skull. Wilbur did not even have time to register the shrill, eerie scream before the hard wood struck him.

Buddy knew it was the most powerful thrust he had ever made with his sticks. Every part of him was there, adding to the strength of his swing. The sticks came down directly at the center of the guard's cap, and the sickening sound of the man's skull being crushed turned Buddy's stomach.

"Oh my God!" Johnny ran up at that moment behind Buddy. The nunchaku was embedded in the dead man's skull, and Buddy was struggling to pull it free. Johnny watched in horror, then saw the remains of Josh.

"Josh...Josh...Josh...." Buddy was in a state of shock. With each tug of his stick he cried out the name of his friend. Finally he pulled the stick free and walked slowly toward the boxcar.

"No, Buddy, c'mon. There's nothing more we can do. We got to get out of here, man!" Johnny grabbed Buddy, then turned him around and slapped him twice across the face. "No, man," Johnny said, his voice filled with panic, "we can't do nothing more!"

But Buddy just stared at Johnny, his eyes blank and his mind uncomprehending.

"For Josh, Buddy. We got to get out for Josh. We owe them now, Buddy!"

From the other side of the yard, Johnny could hear the approaching siren. He wondered who called the police, since no one was around to hear the shots.

The sound reached Buddy also, and suddenly the cold glaze left his black eyes. He looked around wildly, then grabbed Johnny's arm. "For Josh, Johnny!"

The two youths ran like hunted animals through the maze of cars. They both leaped the fence without regard to the barbed wire on the top. Falling to the ground, bleeding from the multiple stabbing inflicted upon them by the wire, they ran to their car.

As Johnny Washington turned onto Olympic and headed toward Alvarado, he noticed that the back of the car was filled with boxes. There were at least seventeen of them. That, thought Johnny, will pay for Josh's funeral.

They drove in silence to Johnny's home. Immediately after pulling into his parents' garage, Johnny saw the squad car cruising down the street. He let out a sigh, shared a smoke with Buddy, then fell into a heavy, numbed sleep.

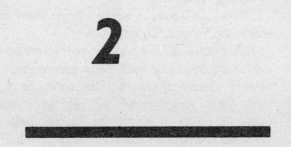

2

THE DEPUTY CORONERS were putting what remained of Josh into neat little plastic bags. They sealed each one, then marked them for later identification. The body of Wilbur Mann lay beneath a blanket on a stretcher.

Detective Thomas Baker leaned over the prone figure of the security guard and raised the blanket. The sight of the man's crushed skull hit him hard. "Jesus, I've never seen anything like this!"

"The kids use 'em. They're called nunchaku sticks. Wicked mothers!" Baker turned up and looked at his partner. Detective Jim Spence stood well over six feet, with broad, athletic shoulders and a slim waist. His looming black presence, plus the cold, deadly tone of his voice sent shivers through his white partner's spine.

"Yeah," Baker said as he replaced the blanket. "Fucking barbaric...."

"About as barbaric as the .38 he used on the kid inside the boxcar, Thomas."

Baker followed his partner over to where the coroners were kneeling with their assortment of plastic bags. For some reason he felt more secure with the other white men around him. He knew deep down inside that the killing of the black youth had been uncalled for. But at least the conventional weapons had been used. A gun and its aftermath was something that Baker had seen so many times that he had grown immune to the sight. A man with his head blown off was somehow easier to take than the sight of a man with a crushed skull. And now his black partner, in that cold deep voice nonchalantly telling him the weapon used and where it came from. It made Baker's flesh crawl to think of it.

A white police officer approached Spence. "The boy's name was Josh Newton," he began. "He lived on Alvarado, just south of Fifty-Seventh Street."

Spence took the wallet and thumbed through it quickly. He found the driver's license and pulled it out. "Sixteen years old..., man!"

"Sixteen and running around with a gang of thugs that bash old men's brains in!" Baker was angered. He was upset because the case was not clear-cut enough. He knew the gangs in the ghettos and what they were capable of doing. What bothered him was the fact that a white security guard had brought it down on himself.

"It appears," Spence began, lighting a cigarette, "that the guard shot the kid here first. The kid was unarmed, Tom, and didn't have a damned chance in hell. Whoever did in the guard got up from behind him…after the shooting."

"Yeah, Jim, I know. I guess I must be getting old or something."

Spence regarded his longtime partner for a moment, then patted him on the shoulder. Both men had been working the ghetto for three years. At first, there had been a lot of hatred between them. The white man did not trust the black man, especially when the black man was on his own turf. But after a while, Baker had begun to realize that his black partner meant business and had a strong feeling for the law.

"C'mon, man. I'll buy you a cup." Spence led the way back across the tracks and through the boxcars. The dawn was breaking over Los Angeles, and both men were relieved to see the light appearing. It had been a long and grisly night, the kind that wore Spence down and brought forth a paranoia in Baker that was sometimes frightening. They were both relieved that it was over.

Spence drove quickly to the all-night coffee shop on Figueroa. The tired detectives ambled inside and took their regular booth. They both ordered coffee and waited until the old, weatherbeaten waitress brought it before speaking.

"Shit, Jim," Baker began. "I've been through this before, you know? Some kids get together, loot, get shot and that's that. We try to protect it, to keep it from happening, but it's impossible. Those fucking kids won't learn."

Spence watched his partner as he spoke. The man's face was pale, and his blue eyes almost washed. Spence knew that Baker felt uncomfortable down here. At the moment, Baker was the only white man in the coffee shop, and Spence knew that he was uptight about it.

"Listen, man," Spence began, "we got our jobs to do and we can't let things get in our way. I mean, there's a fuckin' reason why this shit comes down in the ghetto more than it does in the suburbs. There's people down here, blacks pushing the powder and hustling the chicks and using their own people to pad their damned pockets. Those are the dudes we got to nail."

"How? By working on a bunch of teenage gangs? We're not even close."

"I know, man. It's bad." Spence looked around him at the black faces, living in a black world, and once again felt the bitterness of his inability to break it down. The men upstairs, the city bosses, were more worried about their fucking merchandise than they were about the kids in the ghettos.

The looting of a train, the robbery of a dime store, those were the kinds of things that Spence and Baker always seemed to find themselves hooked up with. While they searched the city for a bunch of young punks, the real men, the syndicate people, were walking around stone free. It was always that way, and Spence hated it.

Coming out of his own thoughts, Spence smiled bitterly at his partner. "Drink up and we'll go file this thing away. It's one for one, and that's probably as far as it'll go. By tomorrow, we'll be trackin' some loser who steals televisions."

Baker laughed. He knew that Spence was right. There were just too many killings and beatings to worry about. You could never get a dead man back, but you could retrieve a stolen television set.

"Gentlemen, I want you to listen very carefully...." Detective Sergeant Louis Bellison chomped down hard on his cigar and stared directly at the two men sitting in front of him. "We're going in after this one, and you two are going to handle it."

Spence felt himself suddenly come awake. This was a chance, a way of getting down in there and trying. It had been a long time since the opportunity had presented itself.

"Now," Bellison continued, easing his bulky frame onto the edge of the desk, "the yard people, the shippers and freighters are blasting about this one. They want the man who did it. Already they've had twelve guys quit on 'em, and that's bad for business. I spoke with the mayor this morning and he demanded us to break it open."

Spence glanced at his partner and saw the tension in his face. His jaws were clenched and he was gripping his thighs tightly.

Bellison moved off the desk and walked across the room toward the city map. In red pencil he drew a square, one point of which began at the railroad yard. "Now, the kid who was killed there came from around here. Considering his age, they got to be a neighborhood gang. I want all of this area between here and here checked out."

Spence almost had to laugh. The man was telling them to search the entire district of Watts. The underground down there would be hard enough to penetrate as it was, but with the area he wanted, it would be impossible.

"We'll start with the Newton kid and work from there." Baker spoke quickly, sitting on the edge of his chair.

"Fine, get his parents to tell you everything they know about his friends, what he does...or did."

Bellison looked from man to man. He was intense and he was shaken. The murder that morning had caused more than one reaction from men higher up in the institution than himself.

"Now, we got a reign of terror that the newspapers and media will latch onto if they can. Get those little bastards and let's put a stop to this!"

"Right, sir!" Baker stood up erect and walked out of the room. Spence nodded to the sergeant and followed his partner out into the hallway. They finally met again at the elevator.

"We got it, didn't we?" Baker said.

"Yeah, we got a chance now. We got a little freedom, a little bit of space to move."

Baker looked at Spence, at the man's cold, brown eyes and his chiseled face. He saw determination there, and forcefulness. They were qualities that he wished his partner did not possess. "You're not after the fuckin' kids at all, are you?"

The elevator doors opened and Spence walked into the cubicle. As Baker entered, Spence smiled at him ruthlessly. "Tom, you got more insight than you deserve!"

As the doors closed, the two detectives began laughing, one a little more nervously than the other.

3

THE GRAY, EARLY MORNING sunlight was streaking through the wooden slats of the dilapidated garage. It was a cold, cloudy morning; a damp chill hung in the air like a sodden blanket.

Johnny Washington tried to stop himself from shivering. He had never been as cold as he was now. His entire body seemed to be without blood or flesh. His legs were numb and his breathing strained. He stretched his lanky frame outward, pushing his feet against the floorboard and trying to get the circulation moving again. Reaching for the cigarettes on the dashboard, he felt a twinge of pain in his arm and found himself shaking as he put the match to the tip.

Then the events of just a few hours ago began pouring through his exhausted brain in a flood of nightmare images. The security guard lying face down with his skull shattered, the remains of his longtime friend Josh splattered throughout the cold and dark boxcar..., the images had been with Johnny throughout his troubled sleep. But then, at least, he was able to tell himself that it had been only a dream.

"Buddy! Wake up, man. We got things to take care of!"

Buddy opened his eyes and, before saying anything, reached for a pack of cigarettes. He lit one, then inhaled deeply, feeling the warming smoke invade his deadened limbs.

"Oh man!" Buddy said, his voice hoarse and strained. "I need somethin'..., like a drink. Your pop got anything inside the house?"

"No. He takes the juice to bed with him, keeps it right there under the covers."

"That's shit, Johnny. The whole fuckin' night's shit!"

"Yeah, but we got to get movin' with this stuff. You know they're going to be coming after someone down here, and they probably found out where Josh lived so they'll be all over the place." Johnny took a long drag on his smoke before continuing. "We'll take this stuff to Sam's before it gets really hot. After that, we'll decide what to do."

"Why'd that motherfucker shoot Josh? I mean, Josh wasn't about to hurt no one!" Buddy's voice cracked as he spoke. The emotion surprised Johnny because he had always thought of Buddy as cold and heart-less. Obviously, there was a lot more to his friend than he could see.

"No need to answer that one, Buddy. Those white motherfuckin' honkies don't need no excuses." Johnny started the engine with a roar. The anger that had been so long in coming was finally surging through him. "But at least," Johnny continued as he backed out of the garage, "at least they're all scared shitless. Every one of them fuckin' honkie guards is probably shakin' in their goddamned boots!"

As Johnny turned onto Alvarado, he glanced over at Buddy. The bulky black youth was staring straight ahead, not seeing, and with his jaws tightly clenched. The rage and the anger were evident.

"Listen, Buddy," Johnny began soothingly, seeing that his friend was rapidly approaching his boiling point, "we'll take care of this shit, get ourselves out of sight, then sit down and discuss matters. Keep your-self cool and we'll work something out. All right?"

"Yeah, I dig where you're coming from, Johnny. But it's fucking hard to keep it easy."

They reached Compton Boulevard and Johnny turned into an alleyway behind the 209 Club. The alleyway was deserted as it was still too early in the morning for street action to begin. In another hour or so the pimps and their girls would be coming out try-ing to pick up on the white businessmen taking an early lunch break. The junkies would be doing life-or-death battle for their first score of the day, and busi-ness would go on as usual on the ghetto street.

Johnny stopped the car behind an old, rotting building next to the 209 Club. He honked the horn once,
then watched the greasy, dusty window for some kind
of movement. Soon the curtain was pulled back and
the moony, black face of Sam appeared. The old man
nodded once and left the window.

"You wait here, Buddy. I'll rap with Sam and get
us some breakfast money." As Johnny left the car, he
glanced back at Buddy. The stocky boy was sitting
straight, staring ahead and not moving.

"You okay, my man?" Johnny asked, leaning in
through the window.

Buddy turned toward the driver's side, stared at
Johnny as though he didn't know him, and nodded
that he was okay. Johnny didn't believe it. He could
see the coldness, the deep churning within his friend.
He was beginning to worry about Buddy's ability to
handle the events of the night before.

Johnny stood at the door and waited for Sam. His
mind was racing toward the possibilities of the meeting. If Sam had already heard about the killings at the
yard, he would try to get the price down as low as he
could for the watches. In that case, Johnny decided,
he would have to go with the chubby, brown-com-
plexioned man for one reason—there was no one else
he could unload the stuff on without raising suspicion.

Finally the door opened and Sam stood there grinning his huge silly grin. "Hey, baby! Wa's happenin'?"

"Got some shit for you, Sam. Watches, over fifteen
hundred of 'em." Johnny watched the older man carefully, trying to detect some flickering of knowledge

in the man's face. But Sam just stood there, smiling.

"That many, eh? Not bad for a young dude like yourself, baby. Lemme have a look…." And with that, Sam pushed by Johnny and walked over to the car. Johnny followed, noticing that Sam stopped when he saw Buddy sitting in the front seat. Johnny knew that Sam didn't like having the quick-tempered young black around when he did business.

Sam's game was selling watches in the lots of supermarkets around town, shuffling up to the white customers, pulling back his sleeves and revealing his watch-studded arms. It wasn't a bad way to make a few bucks, but it was soft, and Sam, with his bald head and his rotund physique, was naturally built for soft work. Buddy's coldness and size shook the little man, and everyone knew it.

"Open the trunk, Johnny. Le's see wha's happenin' here."

Johnny got the keys from the ignition and opened the trunk. There were at least ten boxes stacked inside. Quickly, Johnny ripped one open and unwrapped an inexpensive yet pretty Swiss watch. Sam took the watch and fondled it, then turned it over and over in his hands.

"Cheap shit, Johnny. This stuff's worth 'bout two bucks on the market…."

Johnny watched the little man and felt himself growing angry. His fists were clenching and unclenching. Josh was dead because of these watches, and this cheap little bastard was telling them how cheap the merchandise was.

"Give you, say, five hundred cold cash." Sam stepped back and waited for Johnny to respond.

"A thou', my man, and you'll have a deal."

"Bullshit! Ain' nowhere else you goin' take this shit but here. Either take what I'm givin' or go someplace else..., if you can." Sam wore his complacent smile, the one that most aggravated Johnny. He had seen it on his father during those times when the bottle was nearly empty and the old, beaten man would begin talking about the end.

Johnny thought for a moment and remembered his promise to himself. There was no way out now. Both he and Buddy would have to get off the streets. There was no doubt that word would be out soon enough and they, along with the watches, would be hot as hell.

"Okay..., let's move it out of here."

After they finished unloading the car, dumping the boxes inside Sam's spacious, rotting apartment, the older black man pulled out five one-hundred-dollar bills and handed them to Johnny.

"When's the next shit coming?" Sam asked.

"Don't know, Sam. Maybe in a week."

"Try for some cameras, Johnny. That stuff goes down real good...."

Johnny looked silently at Sam, then turned on his heels and walked out of the room. He knew at that moment that it would be the last time he would ever deal with this little, soft black man. From here on out, thought Johnny, things are going to be different. The fuckin' scene has ended, and there's no place to go but up. A wave of relief flowed through the young black as he took his seat in the car and waited for Buddy. He had always hated this little shit deal, and now, because of what had happened last night, he was out of it forever.

There was no way he or Buddy could ever go back to the yards and deal with people like Sam. It had been good for a few years, providing Johnny with a means of laying some money on his parents and keeping his little sister in school. For Buddy, it had meant that his mother was eating.

But now they were men, and they had killed. The rail yards would be for other young blacks coming up, trying to etch themselves a place in the jungle. Johnny realized as he drove down the alley that he and Buddy had graduated the night before.

Outside his house, Johnny spotted his little sister walking down the sidewalk. Leslie was fifteen years old, and her body was fine and slim. Her pert breasts, already rich and full, were shaped nicely against the tight-fitting sweater she wore. Johnny, alone now after having dropped Buddy off at his home, pulled up next to the sidewalk in front of Leslie.

"Where you off to, girl? You're supposed to be in school!"

Leslie peered into the window with a wide smile, revealing perfectly formed white teeth. Her ivory skin, her soft doe-like eyes were irresistible and Johnny found himself smiling. "I'm going downtown for a while, Johnny. There's a job..., part time, at the dime store."

"You don't have to work, Les. I got some bread for everyone...."

She looked down at her brother with accusing eyes. Even though she loved him more than anyone else in the family, she found him exasperating. Her parents never seemed to care much where the money came from as long as Johnny dropped some on the kitchen table when he came in. But Leslie had been on the streets, and she knew what was going down, and she suspected that Johnny was involved in something bad. The thought frightened her because she knew she couldn't go on without him.

"Well, girl, what you say?" Johnny tried to make his voice as stern as possible. He was the only one who ever disciplined her and seemed to care enough to make it his business.

"Part time, Johnny. I only took today off so's I could check on it. If I get the job, it'll be at nights..., so I'll still be able to go to school."

Johnny watched her closely. Her manner was always deceiving to him. Anita, his bitch, did the same thing to him—making it impossible to tell exactly what she was saying.

"Okay, baby. But you quit that school and I'll kick your black-ass hide. Dig?"

Leslie laughed. "Johnny, you're too much. You always worry 'bout everythin'. Nothin's comin' down that I won't tell you about. I always tell you everythin', don't I?"

Exasperated, Johnny shook his head. "Okay, see you tonight, okay?"

"Sure, Johnny. See you later." Leslie leaned down and kissed him on the cheek, then swaggered off toward downtown. Johnny watched her in his side-view mirror and felt a twinge of remorse. The girl looked fine; her hips were small and tight, and her long legs were beautifully shaped. He wondered how many dudes were trying to put the make on her and if she had ever let them do it to her. The idea angered him, and he slammed his car into first and drove quickly up the driveway and into the garage.

Johnny's home was one of those small wood houses built during the thirties. Two bedrooms, a living room and a kitchen provided the family of four with cramped and messy quarters. The backyard was laden with tall weeds, and the front yard was nothing but dirt. The grass had been allowed to die two years ago, and since then no one had bothered to replant.

Inside the kitchen, Johnny heard the television set blasting away. He heard the raucous laughter of some idiot game show where contestants were trying for the big money. It was no different now than it had been every day for the last two years, ever since his father had been fired.

On the stove Johnny's mother had made a potato pie. Johnny took a huge mouthful and felt the food as it warmed his insides. He hadn't eaten since the night before, and he was starving. He gulped down four more forkfuls before going into the living room.

"Johnny!" The old, plump woman sat sprawled on the couch, her face aglow from the television set directly in front of her. Sitting on the dilapidated old

chair in the corner was his father. The man was thin
and old, his black face drawn with the lines of age
and defeat. The old man looked for a second at his
son, revealing liquid, bloodshot eyes. He said nothing
to Johnny, then turned what was left of his concentration back to the game show.

"Hey, mom. What's this about Leslie?"

"Oh, that girl got it in her li'l head that she wants
to work. I see nothin' wrong with that, though, con-
siderin' the situation...." Her voice trailed off as she
found herself drawn closer to the television. A con-
testant, a little, plump white woman, was about to
answer the question that could win her five thousand
dollars.

Johnny watched his mother for a moment, then
when the audience went wild as the little woman
answered the question properly, he bent down and
kissed her on the cheek. In his left hand Johnny held
two hundred dollars. He dropped the money into his
mother's lap.

"Thank you, son. We sure needin' it."

"It's okay, mom. Buy somethin' nice for Leslie,
okay?"

"Sure, Johnny. Sure."

He patted his mother soothingly, then turned toward
his bedroom. Out of the corner of his eye, he saw his
father. The man showed nothing, neither emotion nor
boredom. Instead, he sat there deep inside his black
self, lost in his own misery.

Johnny wanted to go across the tiny room and kick
his aged father, wake him up and see him move. As

he thought about it, a tremendous exhaustion overcame him and he felt himself begin to spin with fatigue. He needed to sleep, and he needed escape from what he had been through.

Johnny walked into the little alcove where his bed was and flopped down on the moth-eaten mattress. Within moments he was asleep. The last thing he heard was the voice of the game show master of ceremonies awarding a young man a new car and ten thousand dollars.

4

ELLIOT DAVIS, KNOWN to his associates as "the Duke," watched the short, fat black man count out the bills on the kitchen table.

"Eight…, eight-fifty…, nine…." The little black man worked slowly, fingering each fifty-dollar bill gently and lovingly.

The Duke leaned his tall, muscular frame against the window and continued to stare down at the pile of bills being stacked on his table. As the black man put each bill down, the Duke silently calculated where the money had come from, what numbers house had been involved and what the net take was going to be. His cold, black eyes never wavered and his brown skin seemed like marble, set in suspended concentration.

"There we are, Mister Duke. Ten thousand and fifty." The plump man stepped back from the table and seemed pleased with his neatly stacked bills. His name was Amos, and he was the Duke's accountant. His job involved knowing where each penny went and where it had come from. Duke's calculating mind made Amos almost unnecessary, but one reason why the Duke was the most powerful man in the area was due to the fact that he left nothing to chance, even his own mind.

The Duke stepped up to the table and touched each stack of bills lightly. "That's good, my man."

"We're down about twelve percent in the Adams and Crenshaw area houses, Mister Duke." Amos' voice trailed off. No one enjoyed giving the tall black kingpin information that was bad.

"Thirteen and a half percent, Amos. Those fuckin' old people out there ain't doin' shit for us. But we got to hold them up as long as they're turning a profit." The Duke's flat, sharp voice stung the smaller man, and he just nodded his head in agreement. The Duke had this effect on most people because of his massive build and size and his sharp, cutting tone of voice. People rarely argued with the man.

The two men stood in silence in the small, clean kitchen. The room was part of an apartment that the Duke kept above his bar. The Paradise Room was the center of activity for the man who controlled the numbers, prostitution, and the heroin flow in Watts.

Located at Manchester and Compton, the little bar was perfectly positioned for the Duke's needs.

The sounds of an upbeat rock tune invaded the little apartment, and both men seemed to relax. "Amos, my man, don't worry 'bout nothing. We'll take care of that business later. Why don't you just make it on down and take some liquid refreshment?"

Amos breathed easier, knowing that at least for this day he would escape the wrath of the Duke. The little black man quickly gathered up his briefcase and moved out of the kitchen through the plainly furnished living room.

On his way out, Amos passed the hulking black presence of Joe, the Duke's bodyguard. The huge, bald man glared at the smaller man, enjoying the latter's hastened exit from the apartment.

"Hey, Joe?" Duke called from the kitchen.

"Yeah, boss...." Joe leaned against the doorway and lit a cigarette. Duke was putting the last of the bills into another briefcase and when he finished he handed the bag to Joe.

"I'll try to refrain from rippin' you off, Duke. You dig where I'm comin' from?" Joe spoke slowly as though each word was a struggle to get out. Once in a while, some fool would be stupid enough to laugh at his problem. That would usually be the last time the poor soul would ever laugh.

Duke walked into the bedroom, which was the most luxurious room of the apartment, and began undressing. He threw his clothes onto the circular bed and spoke to Joe. "Listen, Joe. We got problems with

Amos. I want you to check him out for the next couple of days. Find out what's happenin' there. You dig?"

Joe nodded, then patted the briefcase slowly to show that he understood.

"Right, my man. You got the idea." Duke pulled a towel around himself and started for the shower. "Now listen," he said before entering the bathroom, "if there's anything happenin' with Amos, just come to me. We'll decide things after we know a little more."

"Okay, Duke." Joe turned and lumbered through the apartment and out the front door. Duke waited until he heard the voices of Red and Pete, his two other permanent bodyguards, out in the hall. When he was satisfied that his men were on duty, he stepped into the shower.

It was only eleven in the morning, but Duke was making himself ready for the only kind of action he really enjoyed. She was fifteen years old, lean in the legs and pert and budding upstairs. He had seen her walking home from high school and had stopped to chat with her. At first she had been frightened, but then Duke had turned on the charm and she had finally agreed to come up to his place and talk with him.

Duke smiled to himself as he thought about her young, perfect body and how it would be for the remainder of the afternoon. It was always like this when a new one came in. They were never over sixteen, always fresh and innocent, and always very willing to fall in love with the big, good-looking black man who called himself the Duke.

"Yeah baby!" Duke sang to himself as he stepped out of the shower. The excitement was already building inside, and he was beginning to turn on. He envisioned the young black, then tried to remember her name. After struggling through a couple he finally hit it. Leslie. The little bitch's name was Leslie.

Leslie Washington stood outside the Paradise Room and took a couple of deep breaths. She could hear the loud blues emanating from within the darkened bar, and she could hear the talking and the laughter. She had never been inside a bar before, and she was frightened and nervous.

Meeting her brother Johnny on the way over hadn't helped her feelings much. She knew her brother and what he felt about her. She knew that if he found out where she had been going he would have forced her back into the house. A month ago, a week ago, Leslie would have broken down and told her older brother about meeting Duke outside of school and how the older black man had come on so strongly.

She would have told Johnny about the black Eldorado Cadillac the man drove and the fine threads he wore. But that was before, when Leslie had still believed that something good would come out of her mother and father. But after two years of watching her parents sitting around the house, decaying and virtually disintegrating, Leslie had reached her breaking point.

The first thing she had noticed about the car was the driver, a big, bald black man who stared straight

ahead without even glancing at her. Then she saw the
handsome, smiling black man in the backseat, the one
who opened the door and called out to her. She hesitated for a moment, then had cursed herself. She figured the man was looking for a whore, but as it turned
out he wanted to talk with her and invite her up to
his apartment above the Paradise Room.

At that moment, Leslie had felt the thrill of being
wanted by a man. A wealthy, handsome black man
had asked her up to his apartment. In her naive, child-
like mind, Leslie imagined the beginning of a rela-
tionship, a love that would solve all of her problems.

Even though she had heard all the warnings from
Johnny, Leslie had decided to accept the man's invi-
tation. She didn't know what was in store for herself,
but she did know that, whatever it was, it would have
to be better than ending up like her parents had.

Now, the young black girl stood outside the
Paradise Room gathering up the courage to take that
first step inside. As she stood on the crowded sidewalk, a car pulled up behind her and the driver honked
the horn. Leslie spun around and saw the chubby little white man waving at her.

"Hey honey, how 'bout a little lunch break? I only
got forty-five minutes, so hop in!" The little man
grinned, the gold in his teeth glinting against the noon-
day sun.

Leslie froze for a moment, then felt a surge of nausea grip her belly. She began backing slowly toward
the entrance to the bar, the laughter and music inside
becoming more and more like a warm retreat.

"C'mon, baby!" the white man called, his pudgy hands gripping the passenger's door. "Let's go do it..., twenty-five bucks up front!"

The darkness of the Paradise Room enveloped her as Leslie moved backward through the red velvet curtains into the bar. She could hear the high-pitched voice of the white man swearing at her from the street outside.

"Hey, baby, what's happenin'?" The words came at her as though in a dream, they were spoken so slowly. Leslie turned around and looked up at the huge black figure of Joe.

"Listen, he's upstairs..., waiting...." Joe smiled down at her, then pointed to a stairway at the back of the club.

Leslie nodded and walked past Joe and into the room. The long bar on the left was filled with black men talking loudly amongst themselves. The other side of the room contained twelve booths and a dance floor. Leslie noticed two or three couples sitting quietly in booths, enjoying their drinks. The young girl could feel the stares of the people as she made her way to the stairs.

When she reached the wooden stairway she glanced back. All of the men at the bar were staring at her—sly, almost menacing grins etched on their faces. As she turned and climbed the stairs, she heard someone at the end of the bar say: "We goin' have a long, long wait for that one!" The men at the bar broke up laughing.

The two bodyguards sat outside the doorway of the

apartment playing cards. As Leslie entered the hallway, they both glanced up. She could feel their eyes
undressing her as she walked the length of the corri-
dor toward them.

"You here for the Duke?" the smaller of the two
men asked.

"Yes," Leslie answered.

Pete jumped up, knocked three times on the door,
then opened it and waved Leslie inside.

Had Amos seen the apartment now, he wouldn't
have recognized it. It was dark in the living room,
with only the light of a few candles giving out illumination. An Oscar Peterson record was playing softly in the background.

The door closed behind her, and now Leslie stood
alone in the Duke's apartment.

"Leslie! Baby, I'm glad you came by...." The Duke
stood in the doorway to the bedroom. His voice was
soft and comforting, and Leslie felt instant relief upon
seeing him.

"Hi," she said softly.

Duke walked across the living room and stood
across from his little black girl. He held her shoulders
and looked down at her. "Baby, you're about the most
beautiful thing these eyes have ever beheld!"

Leslie felt herself blushing. Her heart was pound-
ing and chills were shooting up and down her spine.
The Duke's expensive cologne was like a sweet nec-
tar to her. She had never in her life smelled anything
that good.

"Listen honey," Duke began, leading her by the

hand to the couch, "I want a couple of things clear between us. I mean, I don't know what happened when I saw you, but somethin' sure 'nuff did, and I haven't been able to think 'bout no one but you since." The Duke sat Leslie down on the couch and faced her. Intense seriousness was written across his black face. "Now, I don't know why you came down here, but I hope it's 'cause you think the same way I do."

It had worked so many times before that the Duke sometimes had trouble keeping himself from laughing. Young girls, just over puberty, finding an older, wealthy man in love with them, were usually defenseless. Now, as Duke gazed serenely into Leslie's large, doe-like eyes, he knew that it was working again.

"Well, girl? I just opened myself to you...."

"I don't know yet, Duke. Honest." Leslie felt herself growing hot. The man was taking her over completely. She was losing all sense of herself.

"Listen, don't call me Duke. That's for other people. You call me Elliot, all right? You dig where I'm comin' from, Leslie?"

"Yes, Elliot. I do. I really do."

As he began stroking her fine, brown cheek, Leslie knew that she was going to go all the way. She had never done it before, and the prospect frightened her. But as the big, strong black man took her into his arms and kissed her hard on the mouth, she began to relax. He was smooth and powerful and knew exactly what to do.

The bedroom was lit softly with small lamps at either corner of the room. The large, circular bed sat in the center.

"Don't worry, baby. Daddy'll take care of you. You goin' be all right...." His soothing words floated toward her. She watched him as he slowly undressed her. When she was naked, she felt herself blush with embarrassment, then felt a tremendous excitement flow through her as Duke stood back and examined her nude flesh.

"Baby..., you are the finest!"

"Thank you." It had been a long time since anyone had noticed her like that.

Leslie watched as Duke undressed. She felt herself choke slightly as he revealed his hardened manhood to her.

"No need to be afraid, baby," Duke said softly as he took her in his arms and lay her across the huge bed. "I'm goin' be real nice and easy with you. Real nice and easy...."

Even so, Leslie screamed out when he plunged deep inside her unexplored valley. She moaned and gasped, feeling herself invaded for the first time in her life.

The Duke loved her screams and cries. The young ones were the best and this one was the finest he had ever had. As he spent himself inside her tight, moist vagina, Duke knew that he would hang onto this one for a long time before sending her out into the streets.

5

JOSH NEWTON'S MOTHER lived in a small house that rested just beneath the Harbor Freeway near Manchester Boulevard. Around hers were other small homes, quickly decaying with age and the inability and desire of the residents to keep them up. Only Mrs. Newton's home proudly displayed a perfectly green front lawn and a beautiful rose garden on either side of the badly cracked cement sidewalk leading up to the front door.

Detective Jim Spence stood at the end of the walkway and admired the little white frame house. The roar of the freeway rush-hour traffic was deafening, the smell of carbon monoxide and lead from the exhausts of the thousands of automobiles that passed only yards away was sickening. But even with that, thought Spence, the little house seemed to transcend the blight around it.

Before approaching the black-wreathed front door, Detective Spence glanced back at his partner leaning against the hood of the car. Thomas Baker smoked a cigarette and nodded to his friend. It had been decided that since Josh Newton had been dead only twelve hours, Spence would question the bereaved mother. One detective was enough, and Spence knew that because he was black he would be the one to approach the mother.

The front door opened after his first knock. Detective Spence presented his badge to the young black man staring out at him with confused, painted eyes.

"Detective Spence, L.A. Homicide. I'm sorry, but...."

The young man stepped aside. "Come in, please."

Spence was relieved that the young black was present and was cordial. "Are you related to Josh Newton?" Spence asked as he walked into the tiny, immaculate living room.

"I'm his brother," the young man replied, then added, "excuse me, I'll get mom."

The house was clean and orderly, the furnishings were ancient. Nothing in the small house was newer than ten years old, but beyond that, there was a terrific sense of pride in everything about the place. Spence sighed to himself. Someone, he thought, tries to hold their head up and they get this. Damn.

"Detective, I'm Josh Newton's mother."

She was older than expected; her gray hair was tied in a tight knot behind her head. Her body was thin and wiry, and when she tried to smile, Spence noticed most of her teeth were missing.

"I'm sorry to bother you at a time like this, Mrs. Newton, but we're trying to find out what happened last night and we...."

"That's all right, Detective," Mrs. Newton interrupted. "Noah," she said, turning to her other son, "turn that music down!"

The roar of the freeway penetrating the thin walls of the house had deafened Spence. But now he heard it, a sweet clarinet playing the old Negro funeral song, "A Closer Walk." Spence had not heard the song since the funeral of his grandfather when he was a little boy living in Macon, Georgia. The image of the small band, his parents and brother and sisters walking down the street with that song being played, flooded his mind. A bitter anger rose inside his gut as Noah switched off the old, battered record player.

"That's better," Mrs. Newton began. "Please, come into the kitchen. I have some drink."

Spence followed the old woman into the tiny room. An old stove and icebox sat on one side, with a small table and four chairs in the center. On the table was a half-finished bottle of Jack Daniels.

"I know this don't look right, Mr. Spence, but it's all I've got. Would you care for some?" Her hands were trembling as she poured herself a half a glass of the whiskey.

"No thank you, Mrs. Newton." Spence pulled out a cigarette and lit it. "I just wanted some information about Josh. I hoped that maybe you could help me."

"Josh," Mrs. Newton began, "was a young black man, Mr. Spence, trying to grow up in a world that didn't want him to. He got killed last night 'cause he was too weak...."

"Who were his friends, Mrs. Newton? Who did he hang out with?" Spence knew he was being cold, but it was scenes like this one that always flashed through his mind and drove him on.

"No friends, Mr. Spence, no friends at all." Mrs. Newton took a long, slow drink from her glass, stared at her hands. She played with the cheap, turquoise ring on her left pinky, her gnarled hands moving slowly.

Spence could feel the tension in the room and the way in which the old woman was being pulled. He had handled situations like this before. The black people did not trust the police, and they did not trust each other. There was little, if any, communication between the victims and those who could help. The only ones who ever came out on top were the exploiters—those men, both black and white, who played on their fear. It always infuriated Spence, and this was no exception.

"Please, Mrs. Newton, your son was killed last night looting a boxcar at the freight yards. There were others involved, and unless we stop them they're going to end up the same way!"

Noah stepped away from the wall and took a seat

across from Spence. His black face was set and determined. "Listen man, my mother tol' you the damned truth! Leave her alone!"

Mrs. Newton looked up at Spence. He saw the meaning in her eyes. The aged black woman was going to live by the rules, the rules that protected her own people. Even if she understood that those rules were no longer acceptable, she would not break them.

Spence rose from his chair. "Okay, I'm sorry, Mrs. Newton. If you hear anything, please...." Detective Spence dropped his card onto the table, turned and walked through the small house and out the front door.

He was greeted outside by the roar of the freeway, the smell of poisoned air and the setting sun. It had been almost thirteen hours since the shooting and Spence was beginning to think that this case would be another in the long line of unfortunate ghetto deaths. Just another wild black youth killed, he thought bitterly to himself as he climbed into the car with his partner.

"How'd it go?" Detective Baker asked as he turned the car around and headed out toward Manchester Boulevard.

"The same, Tom. Always the same. She don't want the other ones to get in trouble with the law. She thinks she's protecting them."

"Yeah," Baker replied, then fell into a silence. He knew what his black partner was going through, and through the years had come to understand the workings of ghetto life through his partner's eyes. The two men rode in silence down Manchester Boulevard toward Compton, watching the street hustlers emerge from the old, dilapidated buildings as the night fell over South Central Los Angeles.

The two detectives were virtually lost in their own thoughts when the message came over the radio. It took a moment before the contents of the police call dawned on them, then both Spence and Baker reached for the microphone.

"This is Alpha Two," Spence said in a hurried, excited voice, "hold suspect at point of apprehension. Over."

"Compton and Slauson, that's only a couple of blocks away!" Baker turned the car around in the middle of Manchester, then sped toward Compton Boulevard.

"We got some fuckin' sharp dudes out there to find those watches!" Spence was visibly uplifted. The scene at the Newton home moments before had shaken him. But now, after the call reporting that the watches stolen from the train had turned up on the arm of a parking lot vendor had come in, his spirits were rising.

"Hold on," Baker warned as he turned up Compton, past the Paradise Room and headed toward the shopping center where the suspect had been arrested, "we don't know yet. I mean, it could be anything."

"No," Spence replied, lighting a cigarette, "the dude who fenced those watches doesn't know anything yet. The killing was kept out of the papers. It's strange though...."

"What? What's strange?" Baker glanced quickly at

his partner.

"I mean, those kids. Whoever was there. They sure must have had a need to unload those watches so fast. A real need."

"Judging from the house we just came from, that need was money."

"It always is down here, Tom. Always."

Spence picked himself up and sat upright as Baker pulled into the Manchester Shopping Center. A supermarket, a dime store and a couple other businesses sat in a straight line down the edge of the parking lot. Directly in front of the market were three squad cars. Five uniformed officers milled about in front, one of them speaking with a short, bald black man.

Baker stopped next to the pair and the detectives jumped out and approached the young black cop who was talking with Sam, the fence.

"You spot it?" Spence asked excitedly as he examined the twelve watches lying in a row on the hood of the squad car.

"Yes, sir. I read the sheets this morning…, and they sounded like the same watches."

Baker stepped forward and wrote down the number of the young policeman's badge. "Nice work," he said, meaning it. "Real nice work."

"Thank you." The young policeman was obviously taken with the compliment. He smiled as he handed Sam's wallet to Spence.

"Sam Dole. Eight forty-one East Fifty-Fourth. Is that you?"

For the first time, the little black man was confronted by Detective Spence. Just the build and demeanor of the black plainclothesman had inhibited Sam. Now, he was forced to speak with the man directly.

"Yeah, tha's me," Sam replied, trying to sound gutsy and hard.

"These your watches?" Spence held up one of the Swiss pieces and placed it about two inches from Sam's nose.

"Yeah, man. But what's all this shit about? Fuck, man, I didn't do nothin'!" Sam's voice betrayed him; it was rising quickly into a strained falsetto.

"Where'd you get these, Sam?"

Silence. The little black man lowered his head as the larger black man glared at him. Baker leaned back against the fender of the squad car and waited. He knew that, if anyone was going to succeed in getting the information out of this hustler, it would be his partner.

"I said, brother," Spence began again in a tone that defied Sam to ignore it, "where the hell did you get these watches?"

Sam scraped at the asphalt. "Off a dude down in Mexico, man."

"Really? And how long ago was that?" Spence's voice was becoming colder and darker with each question. A tension was rising, everyone was feeling it.

"Oh, man," Sam answered after a little thought, "about two weeks ago. Yeah, two weeks ago, brother, I got 'em off a dude in Mexico." Sam smiled up at Spence, thinking that he had finally convinced the detective.

"You sure about that, Sam?"

"Yeah. Sure, man! Now, what's goin' down here, man? I'm jus' a little guy makin' a buck..., no fuckin' crime in that, is there?"

Spence took a long drag on his cigarette, then slowly ground out the butt beneath the heel of his shoe. Finally, he looked up at Sam with glowering eyes. "Sam, you're under arrest for murder one. These watches were stolen last night, and a security guard was killed. That makes you our prime suspect. Dig?"

Sam's mouth fell open, and he struggled for breath. He would have revealed instantly his source had it not been for the image of Buddy and his deadly nunchaku stick flashing through his mind. Buddy and Johnny, they would come after him. Somehow, somewhere, they would track him down and crush his goddamn skull with that fuckin' stick! He'd seen Buddy put the piece of wood through a door once, and it had looked like he hadn't even tried.

"You about ready to tell us where you got these watches, Sam?" Spence watched the little man carefully. He knew already that Sam was weighing his alternatives.

"I tol' you, man. Mexico."

"Okay," Spence said, turning to the uniformed officer, "take him downtown and book him. We'll finish this little conversation in the interrogation room."

As the young black cop drove Sam off into the dark night, Baker and Spence climbed into their car and began driving to the police station.

"You think we've got something, Jim?" Baker asked after a long silence.

"Yeah," Spence replied slowly, "I think it's coming at him from both sides. No sweat, though. We'll break him before the night is over."

The old brick building that housed the South Central Police Department was jammed with policemen and apprehended suspects. The first floor of the headquarters housed the main desk where each new suspect was registered before being led away to the booking room. Most of the crowd were blacks— young blacks, old blacks and a large array of young black women brought in on prostitution charges.

"Looks like a slow night," Spence mumbled as he and his partner walked quickly through the reception room to the old wooden stairway.

"Wait'll summer, my friend. Everybody congregates here."

Spence laughed. The two detectives climbed the stairs, made their way down the crowded hall and were finally alone in the tiny, windowless interrogation room.

The interrogation room was chosen specifically because of its cell-like quality—small in space, with no windows and only one door leading to the outside hallway. In the center of the room was a small table, with chairs on opposing sides. A rickety old bench rested against the far wall, and a light bulb with a metal shade provided the only illumination.

The atmosphere of the room did serve the purpose of giving the suspects brought here the unmistakable idea of what it would be like to be confined to a jail cell.

The impression was not lost on little Sam. He was brought into the room by the arresting officer and left standing next to the doorway. The young black policeman returned Spence's nod, then closed the door behind himself as he left.

Spence leaned casually against the far wall while Baker sat easily on the old wooden bench. Both men smoked cigarettes and already the room was filling with gray smoke.

"Well, Sam," Baker began, startling the suspect because it was really the first time the white cop had spoken to him, "what's happenin'?"

"Nothin', man. Nothin' 'cept I'm in this joint for no good fuckin' reason." Sam's words were weak, his voice trailed off noticeably.

Baker rose from his position on the bench and leaned across the table toward Sam. "Now, listen, Sam. You can get yourself out of here and back to whatever it is that you do for a living. You know that, don't you?"

Sam looked first to Spence, then back to Baker. There was confusion in his eyes. The white man was being soft-spoken and almost kind; the black detective had practically threatened him with the gas chamber back there at the parking lot. It didn't make sense to Sam. After all, a brother was a brother....

"Well, Sam?" Baker asked again.

"I tol' you where I got the watches, sir. Nothin' else to tell. If there was, I certainly wouldn't be in here protecting a bunch of little creeps...."

Sam cut himself off. He saw the tall, muscular detective lean his black frame forward.

"Little creeps, Sam? What do you mean by that?" As Baker spoke, he passed a newly lit cigarette across to the fence. Sam accepted the smoke and inhaled quickly and nervously.

"Nothin' man. Nothin'." Sam sat down slowly in the little chair behind him. Beneath the harsh light, Baker and Spence saw the beads of sweat rolling down the man's bald pate.

Baker stepped back from the table, turned to his partner and shrugged his shoulders. "Jim," he began quietly, "I really thought he would cooperate. All the way over here I was telling you how he would cooperate. Now, he's just copping out." Baker glanced quickly back at Sam, then slouched down into the bench.

Detective Spence took his cue and stepped out of the corner and approached Sam slowly. The little black man could not take his eyes off Spence's hulking figure as the detective moved closer.

"Now shit!" Spence began in a low-keyed yet threatening tone. "I listened to you, podner, and I thought we had ourselves someone who would cop out. And I was right. Wasn't I, Sam?"

Sam winced slightly as Spence stopped directly next to him. He could feel the detective's hot, threatening breath on his neck. His armpits were drenched with sweat, and little driblets were running down the front of his shirt.

As Spence glared down at the little black man, he felt the rage that these sessions always created inside him. It was the fury of watching another black man trapped between the law of society and the law of the streets. It was a no-man's-land, an empty space of real estate where only a fool would tread. Yet here was a brown-skinned brother, caught in the web of the law and dealing with the law on its own turf. The man would not speak because he was more terrified of the street vengeance than he was of society's. It infuriated Spence to realize that the streets held more weight with his own people than did society. If society was corrupt, then the streets were downright evil—at least, that's what Spence believed. He felt he had to believe it because to him it was his only salvation from madness.

"Goddamn it, you motherfucker, give us those goddamn names!!!" Spence's sudden outburst, his voice booming almost directly into Sam's ear, almost sent the little man reeling off his chair. Even Baker jumped.

"Please man…," Sam began in a tone that was more whimper than voice.

"Don't please me, you little shit! There's some kids out there in trouble, you bastard, and we're going to find them!"

Baker had seen his partner go through changes like this inside the interrogation room many times. But as many times as he had seen it, he still had not come to the point where he was used to the rage and bitterness he heard in Spence's voice. The tall black man's actions inside the small room still sent chills down Baker's spine.

"Please...Mexico...."

Sam was barely whispering when Spence grabbed him by the collar of his shirt and pulled him up right out of his chair. Sam stood frozen before the big detective, his eyes wide with fear and his mouth hanging open.

"You claim police brutality, you little cocksucker, and I'll fuckin' blow your brains out! Dig?"

Sam nodded quickly. Spence held him a moment longer, then slapped the little man almost gently across the face. A squeak of pain shot from Sam's lips before he fell back into his chair.

"You ready, man?" Spence demanded after Sam had settled down.

But Sam was going to wait a little longer. Whatever Spence had done to him, he knew that it couldn't be worse than that nunchaku being whipped above his head by a revengeful Buddy. Nothing, thought Sam, could be worse than that end.

"Okay, let's get the hell out of here, Tom." Baker rose to his feet and walked to the door. He held the door open and waited for his partner.

Spence watched the relief work its way across Sam's face. He reached the door, stopped and spoke one more time to the hunched over figure sitting at the small table.

"Hey baby?" Spence called out. "You ever hear of

a place in this building known as honkietown?"

Spence watched Sam's shoulders tighten. He could see the man clench himself, as if trying to keep his body from falling apart.

"Well," Spence began after a moment, "honkietown is where all the motherfuckin' white dudes stay when they come visit. Dig? We separate the black from the white 'cause you ever imagine what would happen if we mixed them? I mean, those dudes are killers, man! They'd just as soon cut your balls off as look at you! Ain't that right, Tom?"

"You bet. Mean motherfuckers," Baker replied.

"So," Spence continued, careful to draw his words out in the menacing street slang, "you jus' watch it, 'cause that's where we 'bout to send your ass, motherfucker!"

"Washington!"

Spence and Baker glanced quickly at one another. "What was that, Sam?" Baker asked quickly.

"Johnny Washington!" Sam's voice was etched with fear; he could barely pronounce the name. "Johnny Washington, that's the dude who give me the watches. His friend, man, is Buddy. I don' know his last name."

The arresting officer was standing outside the door and Spence signaled him over. "Keep him locked up for another forty-eight hours. If nothin's breakin' by then, we'll hold him on a selling ordinance. Okay?"

The young black officer smiled. "Yeah, I got you, sir." Spence patted the young officer on the shoulder as he and Baker moved away from the interrogation room. As the two men walked quickly toward the information center where they would file an all-points bulletin for the fugitives, Baker found himself smiling.

"What's so fucking funny, Tom?" Spence asked.

"I dunno, Jim. Sometimes I think I know you pretty well, you know? But every time I go into one of those damned hothouses with you, I always feel relieved when I come out. It's like I was the one who was on the damned hotseat!"

Detective Spence laughed, then held the door open for his partner before replying. "It's like they say about prisons, Tom. You can never tell who the real prisoners are—the inmates or the guards."

Detective Baker chuckled. He knew exactly what his longtime partner meant, and it was good to be finished with the interrogation room. At least for tonight.

6

AS AN ALL-POINTS BULLETIN went out over the airwaves of the Los Angeles police radios, Johnny Washington and Buddy were walking down Compton Boulevard toward the Paradise Room. The streets were filled with people beginning their night's work. The hustlers, pimps and whores had all started to congregate, and music was blaring out of every bar and dive they passed.

But both Buddy and Johnny felt troubled. The day had been a long one that had begun less than twenty-four hours ago when they had witnessed the brutal murder of their friend Josh. Both youths had returned to their homes in an attempt to get some sleep, but that gift had not come easily.

They had met later in the day at Johnny's. And while Johnny's parents sat hypnotized in front of their television set, Buddy and Johnny had discussed their uncertain future.

"Shit, man," Buddy had said, "I don' know what we goin' to do now. Josh is dead, man. An' we can't go back to that fuckin' yard. Your folks, mine..., everybody depends on us, man. We got to get some coin!"

After the shock of Josh's death had worn off on Johnny, the young Negro began to see his predicament more clearly. He knew that Buddy was right, and he also knew that both of them were in deep. There was no getting out, no hope of a reasonable solution. Johnny knew that they would both have to go all the way.

"We'll go see the Duke, man." Johnny had spoken, knowing that the Duke was their only way out. Seeking the help of the kingpin's organization was the only way they would be able to protect themselves. So Johnny had suggested that they just walk down to the man's bar and offer their services.

Now Johnny and Buddy stood across the corner from the Paradise Room. The evening traffic was picking up around the area, and the multitude of bars and dance halls gave the street a light, heady atmosphere.

"Damn, Johnny! This is shit!" Buddy said as he stared across at the club.

"Man, you got your nunchaku?"

"Yeah, man. I dig where you're comin' from. But will the man even talk with us?"

Johnny looked at his young partner and grinned. His smile eased Buddy's worries. There was something about the way Johnny handled things that allowed Buddy a sense of confidence that he had never had when he was alone with himself.

"Shit," Johnny explained, "this man's king shit around here! We're two young studs looking for work. He'll take us on 'cause he'll be thinkin' he'll have trained dudes on his force. Dudes he got young and fresh, dig?"

Buddy nodded absently, then fondled his nunchaku sticks, which he kept concealed beneath his jacket.

"All right, man; we got nothin' to lose!" Johnny started across the street and Buddy followed on his heels. Then Buddy noticed how Johnny was suddenly swaggering with a confident strut, and the shorter, heavier black youth tried to emulate his friend as they approached the Paradise Room.

The Duke stood in his bedroom and admired the lithe, nude figure of Leslie, who was sprawled out across his circular bed. Man, he thought, she is certainly a fine bitch! The tall dark man couldn't stop the smile that was forming on his lips as he continued to stare at Leslie's sleeping body.

The knock on the apartment door brought the Duke out of his reverie. Quickly, he completed his dressing by pulling on his silken shirt and went into the living room.

Joe was standing out in the hallway, looking sorry that he had interrupted his boss.

"My man, what's happenin'?" The Duke's voice was friendly, and Joe broke out into a wide grin.

"Hey..., I thought I maybe caught you...."

"No, man. Business is beginnin' again an' I'm a happy man right now, so tell me what's goin' down!"

"Two guys..., real young..., downstairs want to see you."

The Duke followed Joe down the stairs and into the kitchen of the club where Johnny and Buddy waited nervously. Duke stopped at the entrance to the kitchen and examined the two youths. His mind recorded Buddy's stocky, powerful build and the way he stuck close to his taller, thinner friend. The tall one, thought Duke, has keen eyes. Finally, Duke entered the brightly lit kitchen and faced Johnny and Buddy.

"Yeah men, what can I do for you?" Duke was in a tremendous mood. Leslie had done things for him that no bitch had done in years. It was because of this that he had agreed to meet with the two young men in the first place. Had it been otherwise in the bedroom, he would have thrown the young studs out the door.

"Mister Duke," Johnny began, trying to sound calm and steady, "me and Buddy want to work for you."

"Is that right, my man?" Duke was playing now, having fun with the two youths.

"Yeah, we can do almost anything, you know?" Johnny felt relief with the man's attitude, although he wouldn't let the thought leave his mind that the Duke was a known killer.

"Uh huh," Duke said, looking at each of them carefully. Finally, he rested his eyes on Buddy. "That nunchaku stick you got there, pull it out."

Buddy fumbled with his jacket trying to extract the stick. Finally, he held up the wired sticks and displayed them to the Duke. Johnny only watched in amazement. The Duke looked powerful and mean, and now Johnny realized that he also had brains.

"Can you handle that thing?" the Duke asked Buddy.

Buddy nodded, then released his grip on one of the sticks and swung it around in lightning-quick circles. The Duke smiled.

"Let's make it out there in the alley and see what's happenin' with this shit!" The Duke led the two young boys out behind the kitchen and into the alleyway. There was a wide open space between the trash cans and Duke walked to the center of this area. Joe stood behind at the doorway and watched closely, never taking his eyes off the stocky black kid who held the deadly nunchaku sticks.

"Okay, my man," Duke began, "let's set up a little target practice here." Duke pulled two trash cans side by side, then found a large two-by-four board and laid it across the tops of the cans. Stepping back, he grinned at Buddy. "Okay, dude. Cut that wood in half!"

Johnny held his breath and waited. He knew that Buddy was being tested, and that if he failed they would both be out on the streets again.

The small group was silent as Buddy stepped up to the piece of wood. The chunky youth stared at the suspended board as though trying to break it with his concentration. He held the nunchaku sticks easily at his side, gently swinging the free one back and forth.

Suddenly, almost too fast for the naked eye to comprehend, Buddy whipped the stick in an arc across his shoulder and brought it down onto the wood. The board broke immediately and fell to the ground. The sound of the nunchaku hitting the two-by-four was like the loud snap of a bullwhip.

"Fuck shit, my man!" Duke exclaimed. "I ain't never seen no dude handle that motherfucker like you just did! Shit, that was somethin' else, man!"

Buddy broke out into a wide grin and turned to Johnny. Johnny smiled back at his friend. He had never seen Buddy work any more effectively than he just had.

The Duke looked at the two young men and realized that, if they were serious, he really had himself a find. The taller kid looked like he could handle numbers and accounts, while the nunchaku handler looked as though he could handle anything that might come up in the way of trouble. The Duke made his decision then and there.

Back inside the kitchen, the Duke wrote down the addresses of three numbers houses. He handed the paper to Johnny. "I want those collections once now and again at two this morning. Got it?"

Johnny took the paper and stuffed it into his shirt pocket. "Yeah, man. Thanks."

Duke looked at Buddy, then back at Johnny. "Don't mention it, my man. Just do a good job and there'll be bigger things for both of you."

As the two young blacks left through the rear door, Joe walked up to the Duke with a worried look on his face. "Why you do that? They rip you off...."

The Duke laughed. "Man, those houses aren't worth shit! One's run by two senile old sisters, and the others don't have nothin' more than eatin' money. I jus' wanna find out if those dudes are plannin' anything. If they come back tonight, then I know we got somethin' happenin' with 'em. You dig where I'm comin' from, man?"

Joe smiled and nodded his head.

Duke turned and started to go back into the club but stopped when he remembered the beautiful brown girl sleeping naked in his bed. Although he didn't know it at the time, he had set his mind to have another go at Johnny Washington's little sister.

As Johnny drove himself and Buddy toward the address that the Duke had given him on Fifty-First Street, he tried to assemble the plans in his head that he knew he would have to make. Now that he and Buddy had succeeded in landing a job with the Duke, that part was settled. They would work picking up numbers in an honest fashion, wait for something better from the man but be satisfied with their present gig. But Johnny knew that that was not enough, that everything else about their lives would have to be changed also.

Number one, thought Johnny, he would have to get out of his parents' house. Even though he had come home earlier that morning and slept, he knew it would be a mistake to do it again. He had realized after leaving Sam's that morning that he had committed a very bad error in unloading the watches. The police were looking for the murderer of the security guard, he knew, and the watches were the only evidence in existence.

Johnny hoped that Sam would be discreet about unloading the merchandise, but he also knew that he could not trust the man that far. So he and Buddy would have to move out, get a motel room somewhere and wait until they had enough money saved to rent an apartment.

Johnny looked across at Buddy and smiled to himself. His friend had come through for them and Johnny was proud. "Hey, man, you did motherfuckin' good back there."

"Thanks, man. I was scared shitless."

"No need for that no more, my man," Johnny argued, "you got it down to an art!"

Buddy grinned, lit a cigarette and passed it across to Johnny. The two young blacks were beginning to feel at ease, to know that they were going to make it.

Johnny pulled the car alongside the curb in the five thousand block of Fifty-First, then stopped in front of an old dilapidated house. The residential street was dark, and the old houses sat quietly and orderly.

"This is it, Buddy," Johnny said as he stopped the car.

"What the fuck are we supposed to do in there?"

Johnny laughed as he opened his door. "Man, we just walk up that sidewalk there, knock on the fuckin' door and pick up the man's money! No sweat!"

Johnny waited for Buddy to get out, then started up the walkway toward the house. When he reached the front door, he stopped, took a deep breath and knocked. He could hear the sounds of people inside, then footsteps as someone came to the door. Finally, the door was opened and Johnny stared down at a toothless old black woman who looked like she was just short of a century in age.

"Duke sent us," Johnny said after pulling himself together.

The old woman looked at Johnny, then at Buddy. There was a glint of madness in her ancient eyes, a sparkle that frightened Johnny. The wrinkles in her black skin seemed etched into her face.

"Okay, young men. Come on in!" She stood back and held the door for the two young pickup men.

Inside, Johnny found himself gasping for air. The little house was a mess, with cracking walls and disintegrating furniture. And on every possible soft place there rested a cat, all kinds of cats, from the big alley toms to the little striped house cats. Their stench was unmistakable. Obviously the old woman never bothered to clean up after her little friends.

"Shit!" Buddy exclaimed as the three walked through the living room into the kitchen.

"Exactly!!!" Johnny agreed.

The old woman led them into the kitchen, where

there was another woman who looked even older than
the first. She sat behind a large kitchen table, the glar-
ing white light above giving her black flesh a gray,
almost pallid look. When Johnny and Buddy entered
the room, the second old woman looked up at them
with fierce, black eyes. She did not speak, but only
sat there behind the table and glared at the two youths.

"Duke called and tol' us you was comin'," the old
woman who had answered the door said.

"That's fine," Johnny replied, now itching to get
out of the place. The kitchen was hot, and with the
white lights and stench from the cats, he was beginning to feel nauseous.

"He say you boys jus' startin'." The old woman
smiled, showing Johnny and Buddy nothing but wrinkled pink gums.

"Yeah. Listen, we got lots to do, so if you don't
mind...."

"All right. Always rushin' 'round..., everybody
always rushin'. Man!" The old woman knelt down in
front of the kitchen sink and opened the cabinet. She
reached inside beneath the pipes and pulled out an
envelope that was smothered in cockroaches.

"Jesus, fuck!" Buddy stepped back against the wall.
The sight of the roaches crawling up the old woman's
arm had shocked him. He had never seen anything
like it.

The old woman casually brushed the little black
bugs off the envelope, then off her arm. She handed
the money to Johnny, grinning in a wicked, almost
maddening way.

"Thanks, ma'am. We do appreciate it." Johnny looked down at the other woman sitting at the table and noticed that she was picking at the wood from the table top. He then saw that the rest of the table had been etched out in the same manner, leaving a scarred and ragged surface.

Johnny started backing out of the kitchen, with Buddy moving quickly in front of him. The old woman followed them through the living room and to the front door. She looked as though she was herding them out of her house. The glint in her eyes was strong and seemed to possess the energy of madness.

"You boys come on back, hear? We got some mighty fine happenin's here…, you know what I mean?"

Buddy opened the door and scampered out to the front lawn, Johnny backing out after him. The old woman stood at the door, smiling her toothless smile and cocking her hip outward with her hand placed demurely on her fleshless hip. "Anytime, boys! Anytime!"

Johnny and Buddy moved quickly to their car, got in and raced away. When they had finally turned off the little street and onto Manchester Boulevard, they began to breathe easier. Johnny lit up a cigarette, then handed one to Buddy.

"Fuck, man. I never seen nothin' like that shit!" Buddy inhaled deeply, and sighed with relief as he let the smoke pour from his nostrils.

"That was some wicked shit, Buddy. How much bread we got from that place?"

Buddy turned the envelope over in his hands. "It's sealed, bro', an' I suspect the Duke wants it kept that way."

"Yeah, no doubt, my man," Johnny replied as he pulled out the paper with the addresses Duke had given him and read them quickly as he passed beneath a street sign. "How much bread you got left from this morning, Buddy?"

"Oh, shit," Buddy began, "I guess 'bout fifty, maybe seventy bucks. Why?"

"I was thinkin'," Johnny began, "that after we make the next two pickups, since we got ourselves a few hours, we get a motel room somewhere. You know, stay out of sight in the off hours, shit like that. Why man, we could even call up Anita, and she could bring a girlfriend, and we could have ourselves a little party."

The idea sounded good. Johnny hadn't seen Anita for over three days, and the finely built girl was a keen source of pleasure for him. Buddy, on the other hand, hadn't had a woman since they had gone down to Big Mama's Pleasure Palace in San Pedro. And that had been over two months ago.

"Baby," Buddy began with a chuckle, "I'm glad to see that at least one of us is thinkin' straight!"

Johnny laughed, then gunned his old Chevy and sped toward the next numbers house. He was beginning to feel the ache in his loins as he thought about seeing Anita again. After the changes that had come during the last twenty-four hours, being with a bitch like Anita would provide the perfect tonic for whatever was ailing him.

And even though Johnny tried hard to keep the shit at the back of his mind, there were a number of things beginning to get to him.

After making the next two collections, Johnny pulled into the Palmcrest Motel, a little courtyard of bungalows located near Compton Boulevard about a mile from the Paradise Room. The manager, an aged black man with a powerful limp, had been more than agreeable to sign the two young blacks up. As far as they could see, there were no other occupants registered at the motel and the old man was desperate for tenants.

Once inside the small, paneled room, which contained two single beds and a dresser, Johnny and Buddy began to relax. They had stopped at Burt's liquor store and acquired a bottle of Red Mountain burgundy. Burt was a longtime friend of the young blacks, always willing to give the kids a little of the juice for which he charged them an extra buck on every bottle. But it was worth the price to the young men who were underage. It always struck Johnny as funny that it was easier to score a hit of smack than it was to buy a bottle of liquor.

"Well, my man," Johnny said as he lay back on his bed and kicked his shoes off, "when the girls get here, we can really start to relax!"

"No shit, Johnny," Buddy replied, taking a long swig out of his paper cup full of wine. "No doubt Anita'll bring some fine bitch, huh?"

"That's what she said when I called her, bro'. A fine brown bitch, that's what she said."

"Fuckin' shit, man," Buddy said loudly, jerking himself up off the bed and looking around the room. "What the fuck happens when we get heavy with those bitches, man? I mean to say, brother, ain' no privacy here!"

Johnny looked around and laughed. Buddy was right, especially when there was a new bitch to be made. "Shit man," Johnny exclaimed, "we'll have to fuckin' play it by ear. Maybe we could turn off the light or somethin', you know?"

"I dig where you're comin' from, man. 'Cause I sure got myself an ache that needs tendin' to!" Buddy drank some more and filled Johnny's glass to the brim. They began to laugh and joke about the women they had known, trying to sound like older and wiser men of the world.

Anita stretched her long, brown body out against Johnny's and wrapped her leg across his stomach. Johnny moved up against her warm skin and stroked her back easily. In the other bed, Buddy was sound asleep next to the plump but pretty black girl whom Anita had brought with her.

The night was successful for everyone, and the lights had been turned down and the two couples had moved in the same room. Only the sounds of pleasure had indicated to either of the couples that another couple was present in the same room. Other than that, it had been a very private affair.

Now, Johnny and Anita were lying side by side, their naked bodies touching at every point possible. Johnny smoked a cigarette and stared up at the darkened ceiling.

"That was good, Johnny," Anita whispered.

"Thanks, babe. It was mighty fine...."

There was a long silence as Johnny considered how he was going to tell his girlfriend about Josh. He had avoided the subject all night because he wanted the party to be successful. He needed Anita badly, and he didn't want to ruin it by telling her about Josh. But now, he knew that the time had come and he would have to break the news.

Finally, after a long silence, Johnny spoke. This time his voice was soft and distant. "Josh is dead, Anita," was all he said.

He felt his woman's body tighten and her breathing stop. "What?"

"Josh. He was killed last night."

"Oh, baby, how?"

Johnny could hear the emotion in Anita's voice. Josh had practically grown up with all of them, and he was like a brother to Anita. But Johnny knew that, for right now at least, he couldn't tell her the truth. There was no telling who the police were talking with, and who they might approach in the future.

Not allowing Anita any information was the best way of protecting her. Otherwise, she might give something away, then it would be horrible for her when the police questioned her.

"I don' know, exactly. Me and Buddy went by there

this morning and his mother told us. She jus' said that he was killed last night."

He held Anita tightly and waited for her reaction. All that came were muffled, sorrowful sobs. She buried her face into his shoulder and Johnny held her tightly as he felt her warm, wet tears running down her cheeks and onto his shoulder. Her long, lean body was shaking with each sob.

Johnny's mind traveled back to the day over a year ago when he had met Anita. It had been just before he had quit high school. Jordan High had thrown a sock hop on a warm Friday night in November. The Stylistics had been hired, and everyone around the school had been looking forward to the dance.

The dance had been only an hour old when everyone stopped dancing as they heard the barrage of gunshots coming from the direction of the parking lot. Buddy, Josh and Johnny had fled with everyone else toward the lot and had seen the five young black youths lying bleeding and dying on the concrete. It seemed that within minutes the entire Los Angeles police department was on the scene with riot guns and riot wagons surrounding the campus.

The tall black girl had been trying desperately to push her way back through the excited crowd and into the gymnasium. Johnny had seen her and had liked the way she walked, her long, lean legs nicely revealed beneath a very short and very snug-fitting pair of hot pants. He had left Buddy and Josh and had followed her back through the crowd into the vacated gymnasium.

Anita had fled to the far corner of the room and stood up against the wall, shaking. Johnny had approached her, and she had broken down immediately. She told Johnny that she had been out in the parking lot smoking a cigarette with one of the members of the Black Plague, a local gang of teenage blacks that hung out at the high school.

Suddenly, a maroon Mercury had sped through the lot toward them, stopped suddenly and opened fire on the group of black youths. Anita had dived behind the nearest car and had watched in horror as her schoolmates were shot down one after the other.

That fiery night Johnny had forced the hysterical girl to pull herself together, then had taken her through the police lines and to his car. He had then taken her out to a coffee shop and had stayed up all night talking with her. By early morning, the two teenagers found themselves lying side by side in Anita's bed. Anita's mother had been seeing a man at that time and dropped by the house only once a day to make sure that her daughter was all right.

Since that night, much had happened. Johnny had quit school, realizing that with the constant shootings and chaotic happenings he would never learn anything valuable that would allow him to survive. At sixteen years of age, Johnny had realized that only by making it on the streets would he be able to survive in the jungle of the ghetto.

But through all of that, he and Anita had stayed tight with each other. She was a bright, emotional girl and fine in bed. Johnny thanked his luck every time he gazed upon her soft features, her large, doe-like eyes and her fine figure. With her beside him, Johnny felt that he could never lose.

Anita's sobbing had stopped, and she looked up at Johnny. Her large, brown eyes were tear-stained, and her lips were moist.

"Baby," she said softly, "I know you ain't tellin' me everything. But you got to promise me that you'll be careful. Will you do that?"

Johnny had to smile. He could never fool Anita. "Sure, honey. I'll be careful. I ain't tellin' it all 'cause it's better that way. You know that?"

"Yeah," Anita replied, kissing him lightly on the cheek, "I believe you. I always believe you."

"You just stay with me, honey, and we'll do all right. I'm goin' to make it someday, and I'm goin' to get everyone out of this fuckin' place. You trust me and we'll make it together."

Anita planted her mouth fully on Johnny's. Her lush lips parted and she entered his mouth with her tongue. At that moment, there was no doubt in Johnny's mind as to how she felt.

The day had been a nightmare that transformed into a much better dreamlike state. Everything had changed so quickly that Johnny was barely able to keep his balance. But once in the arms of Anita, he found himself again and was able to relax. Now, only one more run for Duke, and he and Buddy would be able to return to the motel room for the rest of the night.

At one o'clock, Johnny and Buddy dressed and left

their sleeping women. They would speed through their pickups and rush back to the Palmcrest Motel. As the two black youths drove away from the motel, they both felt a strange, unfamiliar feeling. For the first time in their young lives, Johnny and Buddy were looking forward to coming home.

Even though that home was a dilapidated old motor court with no attraction to it except for the two brown-skinned teenage girls who now slept soundly inside.

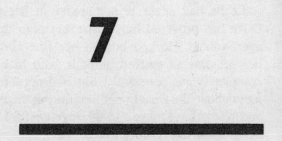

7

LESLIE WOKE UP in a large, circular bed and reached for the massive figure of Duke. But all she found were sheets and blankets. Each morning, for a solid week now, Leslie had awakened to the sweet lovemaking of the big man. Each day had begun with his forceful, powerful attentions. And each day had ended in the same way. But now he was gone and Leslie felt a pang of apprehension at his disappearance.

Quickly, she jumped out of bed and walked naked into the living room. She searched through the kitchen, then back in the main room again. She sighed to herself, realizing that her worries were foolish. She knew that Duke was a busy man and had business to take care of. For the week that she had been there, it was blissful and exciting, but deep down inside she knew it would have to taper off sometime. It saddened her that that time had finally arrived.

Leslie had never been happier in her entire life. Duke had provided her with everything that she had ever wanted. He had bought her fine clothes, given her presents of stuffed animals, and had loved her completely and constantly. She had not left the apartment above the Paradise Room during the entire week and would have stayed in the love nest for the rest of her life had Duke only asked her.

Now alone and without the comforting, totally fulfilling presence of her man, the young black girl thought about her parents. After that first night, she had called home and told her mother that she would be away for a while. Her mother had become hysterical and had demanded to know where her daughter was. Leslie told her only that she was fine and that she would be sending money as soon as she could.

But now, she began thinking again of her sorrowful parents. She imagined them sitting in front of the television set, not talking but just staring as though they were more dead than alive. The image brought a sob to Leslie's throat, but she managed to stifle it.

Duke would be back soon, she thought, and rid her of those thoughts. She knew that she needed the man more than she ever needed anyone in her entire life.

The day passed and Leslie spent most of it watching the television. During those long hours, every time she heard a noise, she jumped up and ran to the window that overlooked the street in front of the club. But each time she peered expectantly out onto the street she was disappointed. Duke had not even bothered to call, and Leslie was beginning to know the fear of being left alone.

Duke stretched out his long legs as he sat in the backseat of his Cadillac and watched the young teenage black girl eating a hot dog next to him. He had spotted her earlier in the morning as he stood gazing out the window of his apartment. Leslie had been sleeping soundly and had not seen him race for his clothes and bolt out of the apartment.

As Duke sat with the little black girl now, his mind raced back to the thought of Leslie. It wasn't with guilt or love with which he thought of the young bitch with whom he had just spent a fulfilling week, but rather it was with cold calculation. He was trying to determine the best way to get rid of her and instate this new girl into his apartment.

It was always that way with Duke, and the man never tried to correct or deal with his sickness. Young teenage girls had always been an obsession with him, and his continuous changing of bitches never occurred to him as something abnormal. Instead, he just continued doing what he had been doing for the last four years.

"Hey, boss," Joe called from the front seat, "we got to get out of this neighborhood pretty soon."

Duke, after picking up his newest addition to his

stable, had directed Joe to drive him to a park he knew about in the city of Compton. There he had convinced the little brown-skinned girl to perform upon him. Now, he had to make his decision. "Okay, Joe. Drop Jennie here off at her house and we'll take care of business."

"Right, boss." Joe started the car and drove away from the park, heading back toward Watts. It was late in the afternoon, and the Duke hoped that he could have Leslie taken care of by nightfall. Then he could get things going with this new brown bitch of a girl.

As Duke entered the apartment Leslie felt a huge flood of relief surge through her veins. She jumped up from the couch and ran to him, throwing her arms around his large shoulders.

"Oh daddy! Baby! It's good you came home!"

Duke looked down at the beautiful young black girl and thought for a second of changing his plans. But the image of Jennie had already begun replacing that of Leslie. It was too late to turn back now.

"Hey, bitch. I got some bad news," he said coldly, pushing Leslie away from him.

She looked up at him with her large, brown eyes, feeling her body begin to stiffen.

"See, honey," Duke began, "I got business to take care of for a week or so, and we got to have this place. I'm goin' put you up with Molly, a main chick of mine who'll take care of you."

"Oh:...." Leslie felt herself sinking. But there was a light at the end of the tunnel. "Can I still see you, Elliot? I mean, if I go stay with Molly?"

"Sure, honey, no problem, baby. We'll be together every night. It's just this fuckin' business came up and I got to handle it."

As Leslie packed her newly purchased clothes into a suitcase, she felt better. Duke wasn't lying to her, she believed, and things would work out again like they had been.

Joe came up to the apartment a moment later and took the suitcase down to the Cadillac. Leslie stood in the living room with Duke. She threw her arms around him, kissed him, then withdrew when he didn't respond.

"You go down there with Joe, Les, and I'll catch you tonight. You dig where I'm comin' from?"

"Yes, Elliot. I'll be waiting."

"Beautiful, beautiful." The Duke held the door for her, then went to the window and waited for her to emerge onto the sidewalk in front of the club. He smiled to himself as he watched her get into his Cadillac and drive off with Joe toward Molly's. Man, he thought to himself, she was nowhere! I mean, she didn't even know what was happenin' to her when it was comin' down!

As Duke shuffled back into the bathroom and began showering, he knew that the next time he saw Leslie she would no longer be a little girl. Most of them came out of Duke's personal little workshop as hardened, cold women—bitches who would work the streets for the rest of their lives.

Joe drove down Slauson toward Adams Boulevard.

Leslie watched the passing scenery—the clubs, the bars, the markets and the motels all seemed to blur themselves in her mind. Even though she knew where she was, she failed to recognize the familiar territory. The shock of what had just happened back at Duke's still hadn't worn off.

The car finally slowed down and stopped in front of a modern apartment house on Slauson. The exterior of the building sported palm trees and a little bit of grass around the sidewalk.

Joe hustled out of the car, opened Leslie's door and waited for the young black girl to climb out of the backseat. Leslie got to her feet and stood in front of the apartment building.

"This is Molly's, baby. You'll dig on her." Joe took Leslie's arm and held the suitcase in his other hand as he led her through the iron gates and into the courtyard of the apartment building. It was almost sunset and the shadows were creeping up the side of the open air patio.

On the second floor at the end of the balcony, Joe stopped in front of apartment number five. He knocked three times on the door, then waited.

The woman who answered the door was middle-aged, black and had obviously once been a beauty. She glanced out at Joe, then allowed her eyes to roam down to Leslie. She smiled when she saw the beautiful teenager.

"Fuckin' shit, Joe. He tol' me she was pretty, but that's too much!"

Leslie found herself blushing as she walked into

the well-furnished, modern apartment. The place was spacious, and fine furniture was everywhere. There was even a huge color television set off in one corner of the room.

Molly was introduced to Leslie, then she and Joe made their way out onto the patio and whispered quietly to one another for a number of minutes. Leslie spent the time looking at the beautiful paintings on the walls and the vast array of books on the shelves. She had never seen so many books in one place before.

Finally Molly came back inside, closing the door behind her. "Well, honey, welcome to the home!"

"Thanks," Leslie replied. "But I won't bother you for long. Elliot'll only be a week or so, and then I'll go back with him."

Molly's hard eyes softened for a moment as she regarded this beautiful, obviously innocent young girl. "You bet, baby…, but for now, we got to get along and I got to take care. You dig?"

Leslie nodded, feeling an instant affection for this outgoing, lively woman. She was so much different than her mother, and she smiled so much that Leslie couldn't help being attracted to her.

"Okay baby," Molly began, heading toward the kitchen, "let's you an' I make some dinner, then we'll have a little chat."

Happily, Leslie followed Molly into the well-kept kitchen. She was delighted by the vast amount of food that was stacked in all the cupboards.

It was way past three o'clock in the morning and Duke had not shown up at Molly's apartment. Leslie sat staring at the television set, her face blank and her dark eyes empty and sad. Molly sat on the couch across the room and watched her visitor closely.

This was not the first time Molly had gone through this type of scene with one of Duke's young girls. As a matter of fact, it was nearly the twentieth time for Molly. Ever since she had been taken under Duke's wing, strung out on heroin, she had become the number one lady amongst the young whores whom Duke recruited.

It was Molly's job to console the girls after being dumped by Duke, then to offer the young, innocent black teenagers another way out. None of them, so far, had ever refused Molly's offer of white powder and steady income for the rest of their lives. After being with Duke, the girls were ready for anything and hoped that by following Molly's encouragement they would someday get back with Duke. Of course, this never did happen.

"You all right, honey?" Molly asked as the television station signed off for the night.

Leslie nodded, then got up slowly and turned off the set. "I don' know what happened, Molly. He was supposed to come by."

Molly felt her stomach clench. Of all the times she had done this, this girl was going to be the most difficult. She was beautiful and very naive. That always made it worse.

"Listen, honey," Molly began, "men are like that.

They'll take you so high you don't ever think you're comin' down. Then, for no reason, they'll just dump you into the pit. It's always like that, babe. Always."

"But I can't believe it. We were in love, Molly. Me an' Elliot." Leslie could feel it tighten within herself, the realization that she had been dropped.

"Yeah, yeah. They always say that. The man is a fuckin' bastard, Leslie, an' we women got to stick together on account of that."

The young black teenager curled up on the end of the couch and looked at Molly openly. "I guess we do, Molly."

"Listen, baby," Molly began again, "why don't you jus' pack it in and split back to your momma's house. Get yourself back into school and meet some nice young dude?"

"No," Leslie replied. "I can't do that. I could never go back there. Never!"

Molly sighed. It was always that way. Once out into the real world, the girls would never go back and try to get a fresh start. They had to ride it out, to take the chance that what they had had with Duke would some-day materialize again.

"Okay honey, have it your way. But this momma's got to get herself some fixin's to help the pain. You jus' excuse me for a moment, huh?"

Leslie watched the middle-aged black woman walk out of the room and down the hallway toward her bedroom. It had been a horrible night, and Leslie had thought of going home when she had realized that she and Elliot were through. But that had been two hours ago, and after thinking of her brother Johnny and her parents, she had decided that she would never be able to face any of them again.

She was on her own now and she knew it. There was no place left for her to go but where she was. Now, and only now, is all I got left, she kept telling herself time and time again.

Molly returned to the living room with a little silver spoon in one hand and a small plastic bag filled with white powder in the other. Leslie knew that it was dope, most likely heroin, and her heart froze. She had never known an addict before, and now she was sitting in the same room with one.

"Don't mind me, Leslie. This shit's for the pain, is all...."

Leslie watched closely as Molly poured a little of the powder onto the spoon, then placed the cupped end in her nostril and inhaled deeply. A smile crossed the older woman's face as the first rush went screaming through her system. "Ah, yeah, chil', it's better'n men anytime!"

The younger black girl was at the mercy of her emotions now, and she could not stop herself. She asked Molly for a hit of the stuff, just for this one time so that she too could stifle the terrible ache she felt inside her gut. Molly, at first, refused, toying with the teenager in order to make her demand the stuff.

Finally, Leslie placed the small spoon inside her nostril and inhaled deeply as Molly had done.

Her laughter was hysterical and high-pitched. The teenage girl shook with it as she sat on the couch.

Nothing seemed to matter anymore. Not Duke, not her parents, and not even her brother. Everything was mellow now, smooth to such a degree that only laughter could express the relief she felt as her problems and her pain drifted out of her consciousness in an easy, graceful flow.

"See what I mean, baby?" Molly asked after Leslie's laughter had died to a gentle chuckle.

"Yeah," Leslie replied. "Fuck em! Fuck Elliot!" Then Leslie began laughing again. She rarely, if ever, used profanities, and the sound of the words emanating from her own lips seemed to her, at the moment, to be the funniest thing she had ever heard.

8

THE RESIDENTIAL STREET was quiet. Only the blue lights of television sets emanated from each of the tiny white houses. Detectives Spence and Baker sat in their unmarked car down the street from the Washington house, watching it for the sixth straight night in a row. Their only lead in the freight-yard killing had come from Sam the fence, and so far that lead had not panned out. Normally, the Washington boy would have been regarded as another teen gang member wanted for murder. But the pressure from city officials, combined with the panic at the freight yards, had forced Spence and Baker into a round-the-clock surveillance.

"Shit, Jim," Baker began, "we've been out here for the better part of our lives. And nothin'!"

"Fuckin' crunch from upstairs, Tom. Those bastards want this case and they'll do anything to get it." Spence was tired and anxious to get out onto the streets. His anxiety showed itself in his voice.

"You know, we haven't even seen his sister. Johnny's supposed to have a little sister and we haven't seen any sign of her. I wonder if there's some connection."

"Maybe," Spence replied flatly. "But the way things are goin', it appears as if we'll never find out."

"I just hope," Baker complained, "that this fucker breaks one way or the other pretty soon. I can't go through too much more of this shit!"

"Anything," Spence replied bitterly, "anything would be better than this shit. Goddamn!"

And with that, both men fell into a deep silence, keeping their eyes pinned on the small, white-frame house for any sign of activity. The bureaucracy of the department had caught both detectives in a bind, and neither man had the power of rank to break out. It would be this way for the two normally active policemen until either the case broke or the men upstairs decided to chalk it up to another unsolved homicide. Either way, it would take time.

As Detective Spence and Baker watched the little house, the telephone inside was ringing. Johnny's father looked to his wife, and she responded by lifting her heavy frame from the chair and moving slowly across the living room to answer the phone.

"Hello?" Mrs. Washington spoke slowly and most hesitantly.

"Mom! It's Johnny!" the voice from the other end said.

Mrs. Washington took a deep breath. She hadn't heard from her son in over a week and, combined with Leslie's running away, she had found herself withdrawing from the situation.

"Mom? What's happening? Is everything all right?" Johnny's voice was edged with great apprehension.

"Yes, son, everythin's all right. Where are you?"

"I'm okay, mom. You and pop'll be getting some money in a couple of days. I've moved out with Buddy, and we're both working full time, two jobs, so there's not much time for anything."

"Uh huh...." Mrs. Washington turned back toward her husband, but the man was sipping on a bottle of wine and not paying attention to the call.

"Mom," Johnny began again, "lemme talk to Leslie."

Johnny's mother sighed, then gripped herself. She knew that if she told Johnny what Leslie had done Johnny would be furious and disrupt the household. She would have to lie. "Uh, she's not here, Johnny."

"What do you mean she's not there?"

"She went off to grandma's for a week, son. Left yesterday."

"Oh." Johnny's voice expressed his disappointment. "Well, tell her I'll call when she gets back. Everything else okay?"

"Yeah, sure. Everythin's fine..., but one thing,

Johnny. I mean…."

Johnny cut her off quickly. He knew exactly what she was going to say. "Okay, mom, I'll send somethin' to you sooner. All right?"

"Thanks, son. Your daddy's in a bad way this week, an' things ain' so good."

"Okay, mom. I dig. You take care now, okay?"

"I will, Johnny. And you be careful, too. All right?"

"Sure, mom. Sure I will." Johnny hung up his end and his mother waited for the dial tone before replacing the receiver. She turned back to her husband and told him who had been on the phone. The old man nodded and grunted once, then proceeded to drain the remaining wine from his bottle. Mrs. Washington sat herself down in the torn old chair and felt herself drifting back into the comfortable fantasyland of the television set.

Johnny Washington rested his hand on the telephone and looked around his two-bedroom apartment, lost in thought. Anita was sitting on the couch across from him, reading a book. Buddy and Jane, who shared the old upstairs apartment, were out eating, and the place was abnormally quiet. They had been living in the place for five days, and each night had been a party.

But now there was something wrong and Johnny could feel it in his blood. He knew that Leslie would not have gone to his grandmother's house in Santa Monica without telling him first. The tone of his mother's voice revealed the fact to him that she had been lying.

As he started to dial the phone again, Anita looked up. "Who you callin', babe?"

"My grandmother. Leslie hasn't been home for a week." Johnny stopped talking as the old woman answered the other end. When Johnny had finally finished the conversation, he slammed the receiver down and stood up.

"Not there?" Anita asked, already knowing the answer.

"Fuckin' bitch!" Johnny shouted. "No tellin' what kind of shit she's got herself involved in! Man, why don't nobody watch her when I'm gone? Nobody, man, gives a good fuckin' shit!"

"C'mon, babe, take it easy," Anita said soothingly, trying to calm her man down. "Maybe everythin's all right. I mean, maybe she's got herself a boyfriend or somethin', you know?"

"Shit," Johnny exclaimed, ignoring the pretty black girl who watched him closely from the couch. "I don't even know where the hell to begin looking for her! Goddamn!"

Johnny knew deep down inside that something was wrong. The way he had seen his younger sister that morning after the killings, the way she had dressed and the way she had looked like a woman—something had changed, and Johnny knew that she was in some kind of trouble.

"What're you gonna do, Johnny?" Anita asked.

"Look for her. I got two hours before me and Buddy make the rounds tonight. I'll spend that time and look."

"Honey," Anita began, "she's not out there just walking the streets. I mean, there's no way you'll find her like that."

"Yeah, I know," Johnny said as he pulled on his jacket. "But I got to do somethin', babe. I just can't sit here!"

Anita watched Johnny as he stormed out of the apartment. The week they had just spent together had been a good one. There was plenty of food and plenty of love between the two young couples. But inside, Anita knew now that things were changing, and she began to fear what was coming.

Johnny drove out of the parking lot of the apartment building and onto Central Avenue. He would head up to Adams, then turn right and cruise the busiest section of South Central Los Angeles. He knew that it was a futile search, but he had to make it. Maybe, just maybe, his sister was out on the streets with some dude. If Johnny found her with a man, he knew that he would kill him.

Two hours later Johnny returned to the apartment and picked up Buddy. Anita had informed him of what had happened. As the two black youths headed toward their first pickup house, Buddy remained silent until they passed Santa Barbara Avenue and headed into a quiet residential neighborhood where the numbers house was located.

"Listen, my man," Buddy began, "I heard 'bout Leslie. After tonight, you an' me can start looking. Hit every fuckin' bar and club in town."

"Hey," Johnny replied, "I dig where you're comin' from, Buddy, and I appreciate it. I'm so fuckin' uptight 'bout her I don't know what's comin' down. I jus' don't have any ideas one way or the other, you dig? So, maybe you're right and we should jus' get out every chance we have and look."

Buddy waited until Johnny had pulled up in front of the two-story, wooden house before replying. "Hey, man, I'm with you all the way. Don't sweat, we'll find her."

Johnny glanced at his friend and realized that he was lucky to have a guy like Buddy as a partner. "Yeah, Buddy, I think we will."

As Johnny got out of the car, he noticed for the first time the old Ford sitting in front of the numbers house. The engine was still running and clouds of exhaust poured from the tailpipes. Buddy was already halfway up the sidewalk when Johnny whistled to him to stop.

"Hey, man, you got your nunchaku?" Johnny yelled in a whisper.

Buddy nodded, then walked back to where Johnny was standing. "What's happenin'?"

"That car," Johnny said, pointing to the Ford. "I don't know, man, but somethin' tells me things ain't exactly right on around here. Let's go in through the back."

Buddy felt the adrenalin shooting through his veins. As he followed Johnny around the side of the old house, he unzipped his jacket and pulled out his nunchaku sticks. The tension and tightness that the young black always felt before using the nunchaku now gripped him.

As Johnny crept around to the rear of the house, he silently wished to himself that he had bought that .32 revolver he had seen just yesterday. The young black had never carried a gun, had never had a reason to. But now, working the routes for the Duke, he had become more and more inclined to carry a rod. It was always touch and go this late at night, and Johnny had begun to realize that almost anything might happen.

The rear of the house was dark except for one light coming from the kitchen. Johnny crawled on his hands and knees to the back door and lifted himself up slowly so that he could see into the kitchen.

Inside, two tall black men in their late twenties stood with their backs to the rear door. Johnny could see the gun in one of the men's hands, and he could see the other one stashing the take money into a velvet pouch.

"It's a rip-off!" Johnny whispered to Buddy.

"Shit, what're we gonna do?"

"They got their backs to us. The dude on the right has a gun. You get him first, and I'll take care of the other one. You dig?"

Buddy nodded. Johnny glanced down at his friend's hands and saw Buddy gripping the nunchaku sticks so tightly that his knuckles were turning white.

"Okay, my man...." Johnny reached up and grabbed the doorknob. Slowly he twisted the knob until he had turned it all the way. He prayed that the door would open when he pushed. Otherwise, they would be dead men.

One more glance down at Buddy, and Johnny pushed with all his strength against the door.

The quiet scene inside the kitchen instantly broke into bedlam. The rear door struck both holdup men and threw them off balance. The black man with the gun accidentally fired his weapon and the bullet struck the forehead of the old, weather-beaten black man who had been tied up. The man's brains were seeping out of the gaping hole in his skull as he flew backward in his chair. The knots still held, and the butchered black man lay dying while still tied to the chair.

Before the other robber with the money could react, Johnny was on top of him, digging his fist into the man's black face. He had caught them off-guard, and instantly Johnny was getting the first punches in. Within a matter of moments, the man's face was being transformed into a churning mass of fleshy pulp.

The gunshot had triggered Buddy into action. He had barged into the kitchen with his nunchaku already arcing through the air. The moment the startled gunman had fired, he had crumpled beneath a tremendous blow from Buddy's clubs. The hardwood stick had struck the man between the neck and the shoulder blade, cracking that bone cleanly with a sickening crunch. The gunman went down instantly, splitting his skull on the corner of the table while his gun went flying across the room.

Buddy stood over his felled victim, then noticed

Johnny struggling with the other black man on the floor. Instantly Buddy tightened his grip, shrieked, and dove at the feet of the man. Raising his nunchaku high above his head, Buddy whipped the free club down and around, hitting the man directly across his shin bones.

The scream was inhuman as both the man's shin-bones cracked at the same moment. A piece of bone from the left leg instantly dislocated and popped out through the victim's pants. The sickeningly white piece of marrow brought a wave of nausea in Buddy.

"Shit, Johnny!" Buddy screamed as Johnny rolled off the fainting man and got to his feet.

"Fuckin' nice work, my man! Jesus!" Johnny felt exhilaration and complete fear as he examined the bodies inside the kitchen. The old man was still tied to his chair, and his brains were splattered across the kitchen wall. The gunman lay crumpled and silent against the leg of the table, his skull bleeding profusely and his neck twisted into a grotesque clump of bone, flesh and blood.

The two black youths stood across the table from each other beneath the harsh white light. Buddy was still gripping his bloody nunchaku clubs, and his knuckles were still white. Johnny tried to get his mind together to figure out what to do next. On the table between them was a pile of money. Neither youth had ever seen so much money in the same place before.

"You okay?" Johnny asked.

"Yeah, Johnny. I guess so. Shit!" Buddy's voice was strained as the young man was trying to keep himself under control.

Johnny looked down at the money, then back up at Buddy again. "My man," he began, "there's a lot of motherfuckin' money here."

"I dig where you're comin' from, bro'," Buddy replied, sweat making his brown face glisten beneath the light.

"We could take the bread," Johnny said, thinking out loud, "or we could call Duke. Man it's a lot of coin here, but the Duke'll know what went down. He'll dig on us, 'cause no one else in his organization uses the nunchaku."

"Yeah, Johnny, we got too many fuckin' people after us already, man." Buddy was already shuffling the money back into the envelopes that were used for pickups.

"Shit, man," Johnny said finally, "it's better to stick with a dude like the Duke. He'll take care of us, man. He's righteous!"

"Call him, man. Let's get this shit over with!" Buddy said as he laid his bloody weapon down on the white tablecloth.

Within a few moments, the Duke and his bodyguard Joe walked into the kitchen. The grisly scene before them did not affect either of the men visibly. Instead, a curled, sneering smile worked its way across Duke's mouth.

"Ol' Amos. Too fuckin' bad," Duke said when he saw the numbers man lying in the chair on the kitchen floor. The old black man's eyes were still opened, and

Duke knelt down and pulled the eyelids shut. "Shit, we'll have to take care of his woman. Remember to do that, Joe."

"Yes," Joe said, standing against the rear door and staring closed-mouthed at the dead bodies strewn about the kitchen.

Both Buddy and Johnny stood nervously against one wall. They hardly knew what to expect from the Duke. Anger or gratitude, it was tough to figure out how the big man would react.

Finally, Duke rose from the side of the old man and surveyed the two dead robbers who had tried to rip off his numbers house. The effects of Buddy's ability with the nunchaku were visible on both men.

Duke then turned away from the dead men and leaned over the table. He poured the money out of the envelopes and made a quick count. "Shit, it's all there."

Johnny felt relieved instantly. He had hoped the count would be right. It would have been trouble had the money been short. The Duke would have suspected both boys of taking something off the top.

"Boys," Duke began, now smiling, "you did some mighty fine shit here. It's been a fuckin' long time since I've seen two young dudes who could handle themselves like you studs. I dig it."

Johnny and Buddy looked at each other quickly, each one thinking the same thing. The fact that they had stumbled onto the robbery had turned out to be a good break. They had proven themselves to the Duke, and now the big man was seeing the evidence of their work.

Duke turned back to the money and counted out five hundred dollars in two stacks. He slid the money across the table to Johnny and Buddy. "Here, you dudes have saved me more than this. A little bonus never hurt anyone, and I'm goin' to do everything within my power to keep you guys in my outfit."

"Thanks, Mister Duke...," Johnny said as both he and Buddy scooped up the money.

"Listen, I want you guys to come back to my apartment for a little refreshment and some fun."

Johnny felt his blood surge. Duke's apartment was one of those places in the ghetto that very few dudes had ever visited. Rumors were rampant about what went down in the man's little nest above the Paradise Room, and everyone who knew about the Duke had one idea or another as to what happened inside that apartment. Now, because of what had come down here, he and Buddy would be able to spend some hours with the man inside his famous apartment.

"Joe," Duke began, "I'll take these men back to my pad. I want you to call the boys and clean this fuckin' mess up. You know what to do with the stiffs, and remember to call Amos' ol' lady and lay it on her."

"Okay, boss." Joe stepped aside as Duke led Johnny and Buddy through the rear door and out around the house toward his waiting Cadillac.

As the three approached the car, the Duke stopped. "Shit," he began, remembering that he didn't have a driver any longer, "either of you want to do the fuckin' driving?"

Buddy jumped quickly. "Sure, I'll do it!"

"Beautiful. Let's make it...."

As Johnny and Buddy rode through the dark streets of Watts in the luxurious Cadillac, both black youths were experiencing something that had only been a dream in the past. They were riding in a Cadillac with the top man in the city, on their way to his pad for a party to celebrate the job they had done. Johnny almost laughed aloud thinking that only a week before he and Buddy were fleeing the police with nowhere to go and no prospects for the future. It had been some fuckin' week, Johnny thought to himself as he stretched his legs out on the carpeted floor of the Cadillac.

As Duke made his way through the Paradise Room with Johnny and Buddy, he ordered Al the bartender to send up a quart of Jack Daniels to his apartment. Johnny and Buddy both felt the stares of the men and the women as they walked two paces behind the big man. Everyone in the darkly-lit room knew that the two youths were being given the special treatment by Duke.

"Man," Buddy whispered as they reached the stairway, "this is too fuckin' much!"

"I dig it, Buddy," Johnny replied, taking the steps two at a time, following the Duke's huge strides.

"I even forgot that shit that went down tonight. You know where I'm comin' from?" Buddy said.

Johnny stopped halfway up the stairs and turned toward his longtime friend. What Buddy said had struck a chord. They had killed two black men only hours before, men who might under other conditions have been friends of theirs. The thought had been working at Johnny's mind all evening, and now as Buddy admitted that the killings were no longer on his mind, Johnny felt the same fear he had felt just after the two men had died.

"Hey, my man!" Buddy exclaimed, seeing the worried expression on Johnny's face. "What's happenin'?"

"Nothin', man," Johnny said quietly. "I guess everything's just changed, that's all."

"Yeah, but it's a groove!"

Duke was standing at the top of the stairs waiting on the two young black men. "What the shit, gentlemen? You goin' help me with that bottle or not?"

Johnny and Buddy scampered up the remaining stairs and followed Duke down the hallway and into the man's apartment.

Jennie was sitting on the couch wearing a very sheer negligee. Her breasts and her creamy thighs were visible. Johnny and Buddy both stopped short when they saw the half-naked teenager.

"Hey, baby," Duke began easily, "sorry 'bout not pullin' your coat to what was comin' down. But don't worry, 'cause these dudes are cool. You just stay where you are and help us celebrate a little."

Jennie looked from Johnny to Buddy with her large brown eyes. She made a hasty attempt to pull her negligee around herself.

"Okay, men, jus' have yourselves a seat and let's talk." Duke went into the kitchen, cracked some ice and poured the brown whiskey into tall glasses, filling each one almost all the way.

As Johnny waited for his drink, he tried to pull together the strange thoughts that were running through his mind. The sight of the very young girl sitting on the couch had startled him. He knew that she was no older than himself and that he had probably seen her around the streets. At first, that was all that bothered him..., just the fact that Duke didn't have an older woman but instead kept a black teenager.

"Hey, Washington!" Duke exclaimed as he strode across the room holding out a glass of whiskey. "Drink this shit and let's see if you got soul!"

Johnny took the drink and waited until Buddy had drained over half his glass before sipping. He had never liked whiskey; the taste had always made him gag. Now, however, it was different. He felt the soothing warmth of the drink, then felt his entire body relax. Up until that first swig he hadn't realized just how tense and uptight he had been.

As Duke sat across from Buddy and spoke about the technique of using the nunchaku stick, Johnny slid into a large, overstuffed chair and sipped at his drink. Jennie watched him intently from her position on the couch.

"You an' the Duke hit it off real good," the young girl said, trying to sound sexy and mature.

"Yeah. Things were tough tonight," Johnny replied, finding his eyes glued to the young girl's exposed breasts.

"Duke'll treat you real nice if you do things...for

him."

"Uh huh. Suppose you're right."

"I know I'm right, honey!" Jennie smiled, then shifted herself on the couch so that her breasts and thighs were almost nude.

Johnny gulped at his whiskey and thought about Anita. He wished he was back at their apartment, curling up in bed with his beautiful girlfriend. But he knew that he couldn't leave the Duke at a time like this.

The whiskey began to take its toll on Johnny, and the image of the people in the room became blurred and unreal. Johnny settled deep into the chair and allowed his mind to wander. At one point, almost asleep from the drugging effect of the alcohol and the emotional fatigue suffered because of the killings, Johnny almost imagined that the half-naked, brown-skinned girl sitting on the couch was his sister.

The thought made him bolt upright and join in the conversation with Duke and Buddy. They talked for over an hour about the various ways a man could be killed with the nunchaku sticks.

9

THE YOUNG BLACK GIRL who left the apartment with the older black woman looked beautiful. She was dressed in a pink miniskirt with a tight-fitting sweater. Her hair was worn high. She walked a little unsteadily, and there was a sheen to her dark skin common amongst people experiencing the heat of drugs—but aside from that, she was a beautiful sight.

"Molly," Leslie said as she walked down the courtyard of the apartment building, "I just don't know."

"Yes, you do, honey," Molly replied, taking Leslie's thin arm and leading her toward the waiting car. "This whole thing's for Duke. It's all you got, baby, and you better take it."

Leslie nodded rather absently as she climbed into the backseat of the car. Molly squeezed in next to her, and nodded toward Joe.

The tall, bald Negro turned around and looked at Leslie. His wide grin expressed what he thought of her. "To the house, Molly?"

"Yeah, Joe. To the house." As Joe pulled away from the curb, Molly leaned back in the plush seat of the Cadillac. Her mind traveled back a week in time to when she had first started bringing Leslie out.

The first couple of days had been difficult ones with the young, disappointed girl. When Duke had failed to show that first night, Leslie had become impossible. Even though Molly had started her on the hard stuff, just snorting it every few hours, the young teenager had failed to calm herself.

She had taken to fits of anger, throwing things around the apartment and screaming out at anyone, including Molly, who happened to be present. Molly remembered Leslie as she would break down and curse out loud at her parents, then pick up the nearest object and throw it as hard as she could across the room, then finally break down and cry.

It was after these outbursts that Molly would bring the girl a spoonful of the white powder and tell her to snort it.

The reaction to the heroin was slow in coming. Molly had figured that within three, maybe four days the young girl would embrace the drug and begin to use it steadily as a means of alleviating her pain. But it had taken longer, and as day after day went by,

Molly had begun to realize that she was dealing with a very strong young woman.

But, Molly had reasoned, the strong ones were always the best once they were turned out. The weak ones would usually become apathetic to their trade, and the white men who came to the house for a little "jungle pussy" demanded screamers and wild action.

The ones who just lay there and took it were what most of these men were trying to get away from. So Molly figured that she would wait it out with Leslie until the teenager became mellow enough to handle the situation. At that point, Molly would take her to the house and start her out in what would become her life's work.

Joe drove through the dark, empty streets of South Central Los Angeles, along Manchester Boulevard until he hit the freeway. Then he turned onto the Harbor Freeway and headed north toward the city center. The skyscrapers stood lighted and shining above the rest of the city, giving their promise, false as it was, of bright lights and happy people.

Leslie watched the skyline as though it were a movie. She looked about herself, to Molly, then to Joe, and almost laughed. She knew where she was going and what she was going to do when she got there. She knew that she would be paid excellent money to offer her young, brown body to white men. She knew that in her mind.

And she also knew that she was developing a habit, finding it essential to keep a steady intake of the white powder going in order to preserve the flow of what was becoming her life. It was all like a dream, because as in a dream she knew all these things in her mind, but her emotions were not reacting to them.

Some portion of her brain had been cut off and did not allow her to take any kind of direct action. It seemed that all she could do anymore was receive— just lie back and receive. It was an unusual frame of mind for the normally bright girl to be in. But as each day passed, Leslie was becoming more and more used to it.

At Sixth Street, Joe pulled off the freeway and drove past the brightly lit Statler Hilton Hotel. About a half block down from the huge building, he turned left onto Bradbury Street and immediately pulled the long, black Cadillac up into the steep driveway.

The old shingled house was three stories high, with a six-foot-high stone fence surrounding it. The lights that emanated from the windows were low keyed and of a multitude of colors.

"Well, honey," Molly began, lighting up a cigarette, "how do you like your new home?"

A middle-aged white man in a business suit walked out of the front door of the house before Leslie could respond. The customer peered inside the Cadillac as he walked down the driveway and out onto the street. Leslie turned her head and watched the man get into a taxicab and drive off.

"Well, honey, I asked you a question!"

"Fine," Leslie murmured, already feeling the pleasant rush from the heroin wearing off.

"That's good, honey, 'cause you goin' to be here

for some time!" The relief in Molly's voice was evident. The middle-aged black woman was happy to get rid of the troublesome teenage girl. She had liked Leslie at first, but since she had taken so long and had been so much trouble, Molly had had enough. Now, all she wanted was to get back to her apartment, shoot up a packet, and give her boyfriend a call. Yeah, thought Molly, maybe we'll go dancing or something.

"Molly, please." Leslie's voice was tinged with panic. "I don't think I want to. Couldn't we just go see Duke right now?"

"Oh, honey! Shit, I tol' you 'bout Duke and his ways. But don't worry none, 'cause you'll see him soon enough!" Molly knew that the Duke's practice was to take a flock of his girls to the Paradise Room at least twice a month. He did this just to show them he still cared, and it usually worked, at least on the still naive ones.

"Yeah, I know. But I want to see him now...."

Molly was losing her patience. Instead of waiting for Gloria, the madame inside the house, to give the signal that it was clear to come inside, Molly slammed open her door and jumped out of the car.

Leslie remained motionless in the backseat. "Joe? Couldn't you take me?" Leslie asked the silent driver.

The big dark-skinned man shook his head. "No way, girl. The Duke's way's the only way!"

"C'mon Leslie, get your ass out of there!" Molly was opening the door on Leslie's side. Finally, once again, Leslie felt herself being overtaken. She climbed out of the car and took a deep breath of the night air.

"You'll dig Gloria, baby," Molly was saying as she led Leslie by the arm up the walkway and onto the front porch. Three knocks and the door swung open.

"Shit, Molly, fortunate no one's out here 'cause you know how upset these motherfuckin' honkies can get!" Gloria yelled.

"Sorry, Gloria, but we got a bitch here who's gonna get them a lot more upset! Only in the right way!"

Gloria pulled both women inside the house and led them through the immaculate red-velvet-carpeted waiting room and into her office. The little room was plush, with a large couch, an oak desk and photographs on the walls of twelve beautiful Negro women. "There," Gloria said as she closed the door behind her, "don't want those fuckin' honkies to shoot their rocks 'fore they pay!"

For the first time, Leslie got a good look at the madame. Her hair was dyed an extreme shade of orange, and her eye make-up was the same color. Her clothes were expensive but didn't succeed in hiding the middle-age wrinkles and bulges. Leslie disliked the woman immediately. She felt that she was dressed up only to please the white man.

"Not bad, Molly," Gloria said after examining Leslie up and down. "She's really a fine bitch. We'll pull in a hundred a shot!"

"That's what Duke figured, Gloria. At least that."

"Fine." Gloria looked directly at Leslie, and Leslie stared back. "Leslie, you're gonna dig it here 'cause we treat our girls fine. And then when the Duke comes by and takes you out on the town, well, that's when you'll be treated even finer!"

Leslie started at the mention of the Duke's name. It was the one thing left she had to hold onto now. Nothing else existed for her anymore. If the man would just come and take me back, thought Leslie, I'll be okay. Everything will be all right then, when the Duke comes for me.

"She's got it bad, Molly," Gloria said in a soft, almost tender voice.

"All the bitches from Duke's place got it bad. We got it bad, didn't we?"

Gloria smiled, and Leslie couldn't help but see the bitterness etched into her face. The black woman seemed for a moment to be on the verge of tears. But then she broke out of it quickly. "Well," Gloria said loudly, "let's get this young filly fuckin' them white dudes with all the change!"

As Leslie was led from the room by Gloria, she heard Molly laughing loudly behind her.

His name was Jack, and he was middle-aged and white. After setting Leslie up in an upstairs room, Gloria had brought Jack around for his fling with the beautiful teenage black girl.

"This here's Jack, Leslie. You treat him real fine, you hear?" Gloria had said with a definite change in her voice.

"Yes, ma'am," Leslie replied absently, feeling the heavyset white man's eyes stripping her.

"Gloria," Jack said with a big grin on his face, "you've outdone yourself this time. She's just what I wanted!"

"That's good, Jack baby. So long as you're willing to pay!"

Jack laughed loudly as Gloria left the room. His belly shook and his face flushed crimson as he closed the door behind her. Then he turned back to face the beautiful young girl who stood across the room waiting.

For an instant, Leslie felt a surge of panic grip her being. The room was small, with only a bed, a bathroom and a small table as furnishings. The drapes, the walls, the carpet were all done in a bright red color and made the cubicle seem even smaller.

"Don't be afraid, baby. Daddy'll take care of you all right." Jack walked across the room and stood across from the trembling girl.

Leslie smelled the whiskey on the man's breath and his thick, sweet cologne. She wanted to collapse, to faint so that she would not be obligated to do anything with him. But that was impossible. Before being brought to the room, Gloria had made sure the novice girl had had a strong hit of smack, just to keep her nerves calm and mellow.

Leslie had taken the white powder gratefully, feeling her muscles relax and her mind begin to mellow. And now there was no reaction to what was happening inside the girl. Once again she was at the mercy of those around her, virtually unable to react.

"That's better, honey. You just be real nice and easy, and everything'll be fine...." Jack stroked her hair, and Leslie felt his hand move down her neck, then across her collarbone. When he dropped down to the middle portion of her body and cupped her young breast, she sighed.

"Ah, yeah!" Jack exclaimed. "That's much better. Much better."

His hands were all over her now, and Leslie leaned back against the wall and allowed him to touch her wherever he wished. He pulled her slinky dress from her shoulder and her nude breasts were firmly cupped in his hands.

As he lowered the garment past her waist and over her hips, Leslie reached down and helped him. Jack stopped, surprised at her sudden enthusiasm.

"You take a while, honey," he began in a hoarse whisper, "but when you get the idea you really go, don't you?"

Leslie just smiled vacantly and nodded as she stepped out of her dress, then slid her silken panties down and stepped out of them. She stood completely naked in front of this hard-breathing white man and waited.

"Oh yeah..., fantastic!" Jack mumbled over and over again as he tore at his clothes. When he was nude, Leslie glanced down at his hard pink prick and shuddered. The heroin was coming on strong now, and she was losing touch with what was going on around her. The room softened, and even Jack's presence did not seem to matter anymore Everything was cool again. There was no need to do anything but to engage herself.

Jack took the black girl into his arms and kissed

her passionately. He was breathing hard, and his movements were jerky and almost confused. But Leslie was so loose and pliant that she seemed to melt into each gesture he made.

In a moment, they were on the red satin bedspread, Leslie lying spread-eagle beneath the large man. His presence was justified in her mind only by the memory of Duke. Everything else had ceased to exist.

"Oh baby! Oh baby!" Jack said repeatedly as he pushed his sex deep into Leslie's tight little vagina. The man was sweating profusely, and he was gripping the sides of the bed as he struggled to keep himself from coming too soon. But his efforts failed, and after only a few strokes, he moaned loudly and collapsed on top of the girl's young brown body.

Leslie held the heaving man against her, turning her head away from his red flushed face. All she could think of at the moment was Duke. With a little effort and a little imagination, she almost convinced herself that the man lying between her legs was actually Duke. It was a satisfying fantasy, and she allowed herself to engage in it as long as she could hold it.

10

THE REGULARS AT the Paradise Room had come to regard the two black youths as Duke's special men, and Johnny and Buddy were treated accordingly. Al the bartender never charged them for drinks but just told them that the Duke wanted it that way. The women who were constantly coming into the place were overly friendly to the two young men, virtually offering their services to them for free.

As it stood, the Duke very rarely had taken to new members of his outfit as readily and as wholeheartedly as he had with Johnny and Buddy. The man had been looking for young fresh blood for a long time, and the duo of black youths who had saved him countless thousands, while at the same time demonstrating their ability to take care of themselves, had convinced the Duke that he had found his young proteges.

But Johnny had been the one to whom Duke had been especially favorable. The tall, lean black youth exhibited an uncanny sense of the streets and a great ability to handle men. It wasn't until the discussion with Buddy after the night of the killings that Duke learned that Johnny had been the one to teach Buddy the use of the nunchaku.

Apparently, Johnny was even more adept with the sticks than was Buddy. And that was another favorable comment in his favor.

Five days had passed since the killings, and both Johnny and Buddy knew that they were on their way up inside the Duke's little ghetto kingdom. They were the youngest members of the man's gang, yet they were both regarded as the brightest prospects around.

It was late on a cold Saturday night, then, as Buddy and Johnny sat in the living room of their apartment and discussed the events that had transpired during the last few weeks. Anita and Jane had taken the weekend to visit Anita's grandmother in Santa Monica, so the two youths were alone. They sat across from each other listening to the stereo and drinking some Jack Daniels, another token of Duke's high regard.

"Yeah, man," Buddy said with a mellow tone to his voice that Johnny had never heard, "we come a long way in a short time. My fuckin' head's still swimmin'!"

Johnny regarded his close friend carefully. The days had shown their effect on Buddy, and it frightened Johnny. The night after the killing, Johnny had sensed a strange, cold calm inside his friend that he had never seen before. To even think that his childhood buddy should grow up to become a cold, calculating killer sent chills down Johnny's spine.

The hit men and the killers had always been other places, older men and a part of a young man's rich fantasy life.

"Yeah, man," Johnny began after a long pause, "it's been outta sight, except for the killings."

Buddy looked directly at his friend and smiled a cruel, deadly smile. "Really? Shit man, it stopped botherin' me after that fuckin' guard out at the yards!"

"Sure, man, I know. But fuck, it's a damn bitch to knock someone off. You dig where I'm comin' from?"

"Yeah, I guess I do, Johnny. But it wasn't like we were hired or nothin' like that. I mean, we were involved in some heavy fuckin' shit, you know that."

"We killed three men, Buddy. A white dude and two brothers, man. You dig that? Two brothers with black skin—guys like us who were just tryin' to rip off some bread. Man, I just can't see where they had to die for that."

Buddy let out a short laugh and drank steadily from his glass of whiskey. "Fuck, Johnny. You're the man who laid that down that night. We could've just split, you know?"

"Split," Johnny said vacantly, lost in his own thoughts. Yeah, they could have split, but it had been one of those moments when everything seemed to fall into place. The opportunity had presented itself, and Johnny had grabbed it. His quickness had made his decision for him, but it had not forewarned him of the consequences.

Although he never showed it except at times like these when he was alone with Buddy, Johnny Washington felt a sickening remorse over the killings.

"Goddamn, man!" Buddy yelled. "You fuckin' look like the world's cavin' in. What say you and I make it down to the Paradise, have a few drinks and maybe a few laughs with some of those broads?"

Buddy was already up and putting on his jacket before Johnny could answer. It did sound like a good idea. Their work was finished for the night and just sitting around in the lonely apartment would only make Johnny feel worse. "Okay, my man, I guess we do have some celebratin' comin' to us."

Johnny went into his room and brought out his best suede coat.

"Shit, man," Buddy whistled, "you do mean business tonight, don't you?"

The two boys stormed out of the apartment, anxious to lose themselves in the noisy, crowded bar where they knew they were welcome.

Saturday night at the Paradise Room was the biggest night of the week. The working blacks, along with the hustlers and street people, all made it by. Some of the people were old friends who had grown up together while others just dropped in for some good whiskey and conversation.

As Johnny and Buddy entered the smoke-filled room, they were both greeted by Joe. He worked as a doorman whenever the Duke was enjoying himself inside. Joe knew the face of every man in the country who might be out to hit the Duke. Screening people was the huge black man's job, and so far he had been quite successful.

Al slipped the two boys a bottle of Jack Daniels as they walked along the bar toward the rear of the room. Smiling, the bartender said, "Duke's in the back. He's got some mighty fine stuff back there with him...."

"Yeah baby!!!" Buddy exclaimed.

"Let's go back, man. I can use a little tonight," Johnny said as he led the way toward the rear of the crowded room. Already he was feeling better. The thoughts and torment that had begun earlier in his apartment were now disappearing. Everything was clearing up, and it would be a wild, groovy night.

Pushing through the crowd, the two young men made their way toward the large booth that rested at the far corner of the club. The booth itself was raised on a wooden platform so that Duke could survey his club-goers as he drank and partied. Johnny and Buddy finally skirted the dance floor and stood directly in front of the man's raised booth.

"Hey, gentlemen! What's happenin'?" The Duke smiled, then drew the two very young black girls sitting on each side of him closer. He kissed each girl on the cheek, then turned his attention back toward the two young blacks standing in front of the booth.

"Johnny, Buddy..., you dudes look like you need a little action. Just hop in boys, and we'll see what the fuck we can do about it!"

Buddy had already seated himself in the booth when he realized that something was wrong. Johnny stood directly in front of the table, staring up at the young girl seated on the Duke's right. Buddy leaned forward and moaned loudly when he saw who it was.

"Leslie?" Johnny's mouth seemed to hardly move and the word died in the deafening noise of the club.

"Johnny," Duke began, not knowing what was happening, "you all right, my man?"

This time, Johnny shrieked at the top of his lungs. Leslie's name bellowed forth, and everyone in the club stopped what they were doing and turned toward the source. Johnny was trembling visibly now, and he gripped the edge of the table so tightly that his knuckles were turning white.

"You know this bitch?" Duke asked, trying to work out whatever was wrong. "Well, just slide in here, man, and you can play a little. You dig?"

By this time it had dawned on Leslie that her older brother was standing directly in front of her. As if in a dream, he had been transformed from just another young black man into someone she felt strongly for. The image had finally taken shape, and she had recognized him as her brother. Yet, even with the emotion she felt somewhere deep inside, she could not react to his presence.

"What've you done with her?" Johnny demanded of Duke.

The big man shrugged his shoulders and tried to smile.

The proximity of Buddy along with Johnny's anger alerted Duke to danger. He looked quickly across the room and with relief saw Joe pushing through the crown of onlookers.

"I asked you a fuckin' question, Duke! I wanna know what you done to Leslie?"

"Man," Duke began, "I don't know what you're talking 'bout. I mean, if you know the bitch or somethin', just be cool an' we can work somethin' out for the night."

Johnny's anger at seeing his sister sitting alongside Duke with a blank, almost pitiful expression on her face was getting out of control. His first thought had been of the young girl he had seen in Duke's apartment the night of the killings. She was sitting on the other side of the man. The question as to what had happened to his sister was now answered, and the answer blinded Johnny with rage.

"C'mon, Leslie, I'm gonna take you home!" Johnny reached into the booth and tried to grab his sister's hand, but the strong arm of Joe reached in with him and pulled him back.

"Now listen, man," Duke began, "what the shit is goin' down?"

Johnny took a deep breath, hoping that he wouldn't break out into sobs when he spoke. "That's my sister!" he screamed, loud enough for everyone in the place to hear.

Suddenly, Duke's expression faded and was

replaced by a look of genuine shock. He was as aston-
ished as Johnny was angry.

"I said," Johnny repeated, this time loud and clear,
"that she's my sister. What you doin' with her?"

Buddy had slid out of the booth as soon as he had
spotted Leslie. He now stood beside Johnny, facing
the Duke. Joe towered over the two young men, and
still held Johnny's arm tightly.

"Listen, my man," Duke reasoned, "this is the big
fuckin' world here, an' your sister decided to join it.
Ain' nothin' I could do 'bout it, Johnny, 'cept try an'
make it easier for her. That's all."

"You motherfuckin' bastard!!!" The words were
screamed out as Johnny pulled himself away from Joe
and flung himself across the table directly at Duke.
His first punch caught the man directly behind his left
ear and sent him spinning against Leslie.

Meanwhile, Buddy had taken Joe and kneed him
hard in the groin. The big man stood there with his
legs tightly clasped and his hand on his balls. He
glowered down at Buddy and waited as though he had
all day in which to strike back.

Buddy was standing across from him, not knowing
what to do. His nunchaku had been his lifeline, but
he had failed to bring the sticks to the club with him.
He was virtually defenseless without them.

The Duke at this moment was lying down on the
seat, with Leslie and the other young girl screaming
and crying. Johnny was lying on the table, beating the
man with his strong fists. But the blows hardly
touched the Duke as the big man just retreated into

the womb position and guarded his skull with his arms.

Time seemed suspended during those first few moments. But when two of Duke's bodyguards realized that their man was being attacked, they immediately plunged through the excited crowd toward the man's table. One of the bodyguards, a huge six-foot-six black-skinned man named Jonah, grabbed Johnny's legs and virtually lifted him off the table.

In one swift motion, the giant of a man threw Johnny against the wall. Johnny hit the wood with a sickening thud, and his body crumpled like a rag doll as he slumped to the floor.

The other bodyguard, a stocky six-footer named Stu, came at Buddy. He looked at the fear in the young man's eyes and laughed. "You little black fatso..., you're dead, boy!"

Buddy tried to run, but the black man grabbed him by the shoulder, flung him against the table and buried his fist into Buddy's face. At that moment, everything went blank for the two young men who had been so highly touted by the Duke.

"Get the motherfuckers out of here!" Duke demanded.

"How, boss?" Joe asked, looking at his boss with the question in his eyes. Normally, both Johnny and Buddy would have been taken for a long ride out into the desert north of Los Angeles. There, each would have received a slug from a .45 caliber pistol in the temple. The bodies then would have been doused with gasoline and cremated on the spot. In the Mojave

Desert, no one would have noticed.

"No, man," Duke replied after thinking about the alternatives. "Just dump them motherfuckers across town. When they find their way back, maybe they'll be more willing to accept things as they are."

The moment he gave the order, Duke felt a knot grip his stomach as though someone had actually buried a knife inside his gut. He knew that he was making a mistake by not having the two young black men killed. But something inside Duke, whether it was pity or understanding, told him that everything would work out.

He knew how difficult it was for a brother to accept what had happened to Leslie, but it wasn't the end of the world. Duke felt that Johnny's outrage was just temporary, and that in time the young man would come around.

"You sure, boss?" Joe asked again as the body-guards were carrying Johnny and Buddy out through the kitchen and into the alleyway.

"Yeah, goddamn it, I'm sure! Just make sure you leave them a long fuckin' walk home!!!"

Joe shook his head, then trudged out after the body-guards.

Duke turned back to his club. The people were standing across the dance floor, still watching, some talking amongst themselves. "All right, people, can you dig drinks on the house?" The people cheered as Al began to set up the liquor.

Suddenly, Saturday night had returned to the Paradise Room.

Leslie watched the club come back to life. She had watched her brother attack the man she loved, then had witnessed her brother's clubbing by the bodyguard. She had felt ashamed and spaced when her brother had first shown, and now she felt confused and sorry. She didn't know what she was sorry for, but the feeling was complete and powerful.

"Hey, baby, you all right?" Duke asked her.

"I need somethin', Duke. Please, I need it real bad!"

Duke smiled. "Sure, baby, Duke'll fix you. He always does, don't he?"

Leslie nodded. Duke leaned down and kissed her gently on the cheek.

Joe drove the Cadillac speedily through the Saturday night crowds of Los Angeles. He took Manchester Boulevard straight through the center of the city, finally ending up at Hermosa Beach. When he reached the first public parking lot, he turned into the expansive area and stopped the car. The two bodyguards sat with Johnny and Buddy in the backseat.

"This is it, men," Joe said slowly.

"Yeah, baby," Jonah replied. "I still think we comin' from the wrong way, Joe. You dig what I'm sayin'?"

"I can dig it, man," Joe replied. "But this is the shit the Duke laid down, and there's nothin' we can do about it."

Both Johnny and Buddy were conscious by now, and they listened with thumping hearts to the conversation in the car. Johnny knew that, after his attack on the Duke, he had put his life in jeopardy He didn't care any more about that, he thought. But he desperately wanted to remain alive so that somehow he could get back at the big man who had caused his sister so much harm.

Now, that was the only thing he was living for.

"Shit, man," Jonah continued, "these dudes are goin' to lay some heavy shit on Duke. We ought to do the man a favor, Joe. Save him from future hassle...."

"I know," Joe replied, "the man's makin' a big mistake. Anybody could have told him that. But he got to have his reasons, an' he was never wrong before."

"There's always a first time, Joe. Always." Jonah had wanted badly to kill the two young dudes who had been such a hit with the Duke. Besides being dangerous, they were competition, and the huge black man hated competition.

"Well, man," Joe said, "get these fuckers outta here and let's make it!" The night had been long, and Joe's temper was running short. Before the incident at the club, he had set himself up with a fine-looking bitch. But Johnny and Buddy had caused his plans to be abandoned, and Joe hated them for that.

"Okay, fuckers! Split!" Jonah opened the door and slid out. He took Buddy with him and dumped the stocky young black onto the concrete. Johnny came next, being pushed across the seat by Stu and dumped alongside his friend. Before either boy could regain his senses, Joe was screeching away into the night.

"Shit, Buddy, you all right, man?" Johnny asked.

Buddy was lying face down on the concrete. Blood was pouring from his nose and his eyes were swollen. He groaned once, then sat up. "Yeah, Johnny, I think so."

"I wish you had brought those fuckin' nunchaku sticks. Man, what a drag." Johnny was rubbing the side of his face where he had slammed into the wall. His jawbone felt sore as hell, and he could barely close his mouth.

"I'm sorry, man," Buddy said, "about Leslie. Shit, man, that's a fuckin' bummer!"

Johnny got to his feet, holding himself erect as the ground swirled around him. Finally, he was stable. "C'mon, man, we got to get outta here. The fuzz are still lookin' for us. We got to get back to the apartment."

After helping Buddy to his feet, the two black youths began walking across the parking lot. Suddenly, Johnny stopped and turned back toward the ocean. "You know, Buddy," he began in a quiet voice, "I haven't seen the ocean in ten fuckin' years."

"Yeah," Buddy replied, "I remember the day. We felt like fuckin' assholes out there. All those honkies tryin' to get their skin like ours. That was too much!"

Johnny laughed bitterly. "C'mon man, let's go. We got a long night ahead of us."

They retraced the route that Joe had taken in bringing them out to the beach. Walking along Manchester, they followed the back alleys, staying always off the main, well-lit street. Whenever they saw a car, they would duck behind anything available and wait for the passing car to get out of their sight. They stumbled and they cursed their way through the miles and miles of endless alleyways, seeming always that they would never reach their destination.

Finally, after five hours of walking, they reached the Harbor Freeway. They stood under the Manchester overpass and took a smoke.

"My feet are fallin' off, man," Buddy complained as he rubbed the bottom of his feet.

"Yeah, I know, man," Johnny replied, drawing heavily on his cigarette. "But we got to figure where we goin'. I mean, Duke knows where we live, don't he? And what happens if Joe and the other two decided that we should be killed? I don't know...."

"I do," Buddy said, "'cause if I don't fall into a bed pretty soon, I'm gonna die anyway."

"Okay," Johnny agreed, "let's make it back to the fuckin' pad, an' we'll figure out things tonight."

Buddy knew what Johnny was talking about. He knew that the situation was not going to be left alone by his good friend. What Duke had done to them was one thing, but what he had done to Leslie was another altogether. Johnny was out for revenge, Buddy realized, and he wouldn't stop until he got it. The idea frightened Buddy, but he felt loyal to his friend and knew that he would have to stick by him, no matter how crazy he got.

They walked as the sun rose in the east of Los Angeles. It was a cold, cloudy morning, and by the time the two young black men staggered up the stairs to their apartment, they were weary and exhausted.

While the rest of Los Angeles was either sleeping or preparing to attend church services, Buddy and Johnny climbed gratefully into their beds. Buddy fell asleep instantly without undressing.

But Johnny lay stone still on his bed, staring up at the ceiling. His mind was still working furiously, trying to figure out a way to get his sister back and to pay Duke the debt he now owed him.

It was now dark, and Johnny opened his eyes slowly and saw Anita standing over him. She had a worried look on her face.

"What happened, Johnny?"

"Nothin', babe," Johnny answered, still groggy from sleep and in need of a good meal. "Just go into the kitchen there and fix some food, okay?"

"Sure, honey, whatever you say. Eggs, bacon and toast all right?"

"Uh huh. Sounds fine." Johnny started to get off the bed, but his muscles had tightened so badly that he was almost paralyzed. Anita watched him intensely, fear growing stronger in her eyes.

"Oh baby, what did they do to you?"

"A little trouble, Anita. That's all you have to know. Now go fix the food. Me an' Buddy are starving!"

Anita leaned down and kissed him on the forehead, then turned and walked out of the room. Johnny struggled with his sore and aching body. He finally managed to pull himself into a sitting position, then swing his legs around and stand up next to the bed. The aches were severe, but he knew that nothing was broken.

Buddy was already sitting at the kitchen table drinking a hot cup of coffee. He tried to smile at Johnny, but his face just twisted up into a grotesque mask.

"Man," Johnny said jokingly, "you do look wasted!"

"If I look bad, Johnny, then you must look like hell!" The two laughed as Johnny took his seat across from Buddy.

"Where's your chick, Buddy?" Johnny asked.

"She's staying out in Santa Monica, man. Another couple of days, ain't that right, Anita?"

Anita flipped an egg in the frying pan before answering. "Yeah, Jane loved it there. She wants us all to go out there for a while, you know, and spend some time."

Johnny jumped at the idea. It would be a perfect place for him and Buddy to hide out. No one knew it existed except for Anita and Buddy. No one would know where they were while he and Buddy carried through the plan that had developed in his mind throughout the long morning hours. "Beautiful, let's make it out there. Me an' Buddy do need a little vacation!"

"Oh, Johnny, you mean it?" Anita was excited; she had wanted to ask Johnny about going out there but was afraid that he would turn her down. "Really, Johnny! You an' me, Buddy and Jane! We'll have ourselves a regular ball!"

"Sure, Anita! It'll be a gas!" Johnny glanced quickly at Buddy as Anita wrapped her arms around his neck. Their eyes met, and both men knew that there were other things coming down besides a vacation. Johnny then turned back to Anita and hugged her playfully. He felt sorry because he knew that it would be a long time, and a lot of luck, before the two of them would really be able to take a vacation and just have some fun.

But Anita had always wanted to see San Francisco, and Johnny decided that after he had taken care of his business, he would make sure she got to the city by the bay. Maybe, he thought, maybe take Leslie up, too.

Even though Johnny and Buddy were bruised, the threesome riding in the old Buick across town toward Santa Monica looked to all intents and purposes like a very happy group of teenagers out for a Sunday ride. As a matter of fact, the three were happy inside the spacious confines of the old car. Anita had turned on a rock station and all three were singing along to the song.

As Johnny sang, he watched the passing scenery of South Central Los Angeles. It seemed to hit him during the moments when the music was playing. He had come so far, and yet he had gotten nowhere. As he looked about him, he realized that everything was still the same. The buildings were still there, the music coming over the radio, everything.

People were probably sitting around throughout the city having a peaceful Sunday morning, looking forward to something in the future that did not involve killing and danger. As he looked at Anita and Buddy singing happily, he felt more alone than he had in his entire life.

Anita's grandmother's house was a little white shack located in the old Venice canal district, about a block from the ocean. What once were the dreams of the city of Venice to emulate the canals of the Italian city were now nothing more than mossy, stagnant ribbons of smelly and turgid ocean water. Lining the decrepit canals were little houses much like Anita's grandmother's. And each house was as degenerated as the canals themselves.

"Well, there's her place over there!" Anita pointed excitedly to the little house as she edged the large Buick over a small arched bridge. She turned right after that and pulled up to the front of the house, parking the car on the dirt.

"This is goin' to be fun! We'll go down to the beach, and then they got this amusement section..., games and things that we can go play at night!" Anita was like a little girl; her eyes were lit with excitement.

"No shit, baby?" Johnny said as he got out of the car. He was trying his best to sound excited, but the plans that had been forming in his mind and the memory of his sister sitting next to the Duke only hours ago were still embedded in his mind.

The three walked into the house. When Jane saw Buddy, she got excited and ran across the tiny living room and threw her arms around him. Johnny laughed when he saw Buddy smiling in embarrassmentd.

"Hey, my man," Johnny said teasingly, "you do remember that night at the motel, don't you?"

"Oh, Johnny!" Jane protested but with a big smile on her face.

"C'mon, I want you to meet Grandma!" Anita led them through the small, two-bedroom house and out the back door. There, an old white-haired woman sat on a rocking chair with an easel in front of her. She was painting a picture of the canal that stretched out in front of her. The painting was so much more beautiful than the canal itself that Johnny could hardly recognize it.

Anita introduced the old, wrinkled black woman to Buddy and Johnny. When the old woman smiled, she revealed her gums. There were no teeth.

Johnny liked the old woman instantly, more because of her painting than anything else. "I sure do dig this picture, ma'am!" he said with conviction.

The old woman grinned broadly. "Why, thank you a lot, son. It ain't but half through yet, but if you kids stay on long 'nough, I'll sure give it to you."

"Thank you; I'd dig that!" Johnny replied, then knelt down and kissed the old woman on the cheek. Anita made some joke about being jealous, and everyone broke out laughing. The old woman sat there chuckling loudly and slapping her knees.

The laughter and happy mood had continued through dinner, which consisted of old-fashioned grits and vegetables prepared by Anita's grandmother. It had continued through the evening when the happy

young couples had joined other teenagers on the Santa
Monica pier. There they played the games at the
arcades, and when Anita and Jane had finally begged,
Johnny and Buddy had consented to ride the old-fashioned merry-go-round.

On the way home, Johnny bought everybody some
cotton candy. But once Johnny reached the little house
by the canal, he suddenly become morose and serious.

"I need the keys to the Buick, Anita," he said
directly.

"Johnny, where you goin'?" Anita was already
reaching into her purse for the keys.

"Me an' Buddy got some business to attend to,
baby. We'll be back in a couple of hours."

Anita glanced at Jane, then finally handed the keys
over to Johnny. "Please," she began, then stopped as
Johnny jumped into the front seat, with Buddy getting in on the passenger side.

The happy evening ended abruptly for the two
teenage girls, and both were in a state of confusion
as they walked back into the little house.

The Sunday night traffic was light as Johnny
pushed the Buick across town toward Watts. Buddy
rode in silence for a long time, but as they approached
the ghetto district, he finally spoke.

"All right, my man. What's happenin'?"

Johnny glanced at his friend, lit a cigarette, then
spoke slowly and with a coldness to his voice that
Buddy had not heard before. "We goin' start payin'

Duke back where it hurts him most."

"What're you sayin'?" Buddy asked.

"I'm sayin'," Johnny began, "that we goin' knock off the man's numbers houses one by one. We're gonna clean the bastard out as fast as possible. Then when we got ourselves enough cash to live on for a while, we're gonna get Leslie outta there and all of us are gonna head to Frisco. That's what I'm sayin', man."

"I dig where you're comin' from, man. But how we gonna hit the fuckin' houses without weapons?"

"Your nunchaku's back at the apartment, right?"

Buddy hesitated before replying. "Yeah, it's back there under the bed."

"Okay," Johnny smiled, "and I'll get myself a rod. I would use the nunchaku, but I want a fuckin' gun for this one. You dig?"

"Shit, Johnny. We got ourselves a fuckin' long way to go...." Buddy fell into silence. He had been anticipating something like this from his friend, and now that it had finally come, he wasn't sure how to take it. Taking on Duke and his men was a little more than Buddy had had in mind.

But once again, no matter what the young black's thoughts were, his devotion to Johnny overruled him. "I'm with you all the way, Johnny," Buddy said after a long silence.

Johnny turned to his friend and smiled. "Thanks, Buddy," he said sincerely. "Ain't many fuckin' dudes left like you in the world!"

Buddy grinned back, and the two teenage black

men hooked thumbs and shook hands as if they were about to start a friendly game of football.

After stopping off at the apartment and picking up the nunchaku sticks, Johnny drove toward Fifty-Second Street and turned left on Adams Boulevard. In another moment, he was pulling into a dark alleyway behind Wally's Gun and Ammo shop.

Johnny left the car running with the headlights off as both boys jumped out and approached the rear entrance to the shop. There was an iron gate padlocked across the wood door. Johnny looked at Buddy and did not need to say anything.

The nunchaku sticks fit nicely between the padlock and the gate. Buddy was silent for a moment as he held both ends of the stick. Finally he cried out as he pulled with all his muscle against the lock. The steel snapped against the wood and pulled the frame right off the wall.

"Beautiful, man. Always beautiful!" Johnny said as he pulled the gate open. Now, all that stood between them and the store was the back door.

"Okay, my man," Johnny whispered to Buddy, "just one more time and we're home free!"

This time, Buddy slid the stick between the doorknob and the frame. Without hesitating, he yanked back and snapped the knob and its lock right out of the soft wood door. The gun store was theirs for the taking as the shattered door swung open.

The two youths fled into the store. Johnny broke a glass case and pulled out a .357 magnum, then took three boxes of cartridges. The weight of the gun plus the presence of the shells sent chills up his spine. Finally, he thought as he and Buddy ran back to the car, I'm ready to get the Duke.

As they sped away from the store, they talked excitedly about the robbery. The one thing that had upset both of them was the fact that there had not been an alarm. Johnny feared that the alarm was a silent one, rigged directly to the South Central police station. His fears were not unfounded, as a squad car was already being dispatched to the scene.

But Johnny and Buddy had fled fast enough so that they were out of the vicinity. Buddy knew exactly where to drive. They had both been there twice a night for the last couple of weeks, picking up the numbers take for Duke.

As Buddy slowed the car down in front of the dilapidated little house occupied by the two senile old ladies, Johnny loaded his magnum. He knew he wouldn't need it now, but he was beginning to feel comfortable with the gun.

"It's gonna be a gas to knock over these old hags!" Buddy declared as he jumped out of the driver's seat with his nunchaku stick flashing.

"It ain't gonna be much of a take, bro', but by the time we finish with the fuckin' route, we'll have some real cash!"

Johnny and Buddy walked quickly up the walkway that they had first used many days ago when both had been honored and pleased to be collecting for the Duke. But the times had changed that, and now they were going after the man's money.

The two old women let the collectors into the house without any argument. As far as they were concerned, everything was still as normal as it always was.

As the saner of the sisters fished out the envelope from beneath the kitchen sink, Johnny looked around the roach-infested house and realized that it would be the last time in his life he would ever have to enter the decrepit place. As he glanced at Buddy, he realized that Buddy also was feeling the relief.

"There you are," the old woman said, smiling wickedly behind her black, wrinkled face. "You boys like a li'l taste?"

"Nope. We got to hustle...," Johnny said, backing out of the house as he had done every time they had collected. The old woman was worse than a leech, and once she got a hold, there was no letting go.

"Shit," Buddy said as they drove away. "It's fuckin' worth it knocking off the Duke's houses just so's we don't have to make that place again!"

"My man," Johnny replied, fondling the white envelopes on his lap, "I dig where you're comin' from!"

They drove the route as usual and managed to collect from seven more houses. The Duke had not even bothered to get the word out yet since it had never crossed his mind that Johnny would be so bold as to attempt to rip him off. The usual people were inside the houses, and the rip-off was going easier than expected.

"Man!" Johnny began as Buddy pulled up to the

final house on the route. "This shit's too fuckin' easy!
I don't know...."

"Don't sweat, bro', 'cause we jus' movin' too
fuckin' fast for Duke. Ain' no other explanation to
it!"

But Johnny was worried. They had been doing the
route now for at least an hour, and it was entirely possible that during that time someone had called or the
Duke had called one of the houses. If that had happened, then they would be in real trouble.

"Let's just make it easy on this one," Johnny said
as they climbed out of the car. "We'll make it around
the back first and just check it out."

Buddy nodded, then followed Johnny to the rear of
the old house. The freeway was nearby, and the
sounds of trucks bringing their wares into the city to
the north filled the night.

As Johnny crept along the side of the house, he
gripped his heavy pistol firmly in his hand. Tension
had gripped his back, and his sore muscles were
already aching.

"What's happenin'?" Buddy asked as Johnny
peered into the kitchen window.

Inside the kitchen, there were rows of adding
machines sitting on a table along the wall. Two old
men were stuffing envelopes with money. Everything
looked as it should have.

"Nothin's happenin', Buddy," Johnny whispered.
"But get yourself ready for anything, all right?"

"I dig it, Johnny," Buddy replied, clutching at his
nunchaku.

Johnny stood up straight and headed toward the rear door. He knocked three times and soon the door opened. Dave, the old black man who ran the house, faced Johnny.

"Hey, Johnny, what's happenin'?" Dave asked.

Instantly, Johnny was alerted. Dave was sweating profusely, and his eyes were darting off to his left as though he expected something to jump out of the woodwork.

"Not much, babe," Johnny replied, gripping his magnum tightly beneath his jacket.

"Okay, fuckers, up against the wall!" The command came from behind Buddy. Instantly, Buddy whipped around and slashed at the black man's face with his hardwood stick. Stu was the smaller of the two body-guards, and as he went down beneath the skull-crushing blow, he screamed a scream that was not human.

Johnny heard Jonah, the huge black man, trying to get by Dave inside the kitchen. Instantly, Johnny slammed the back door closed and fired twice through the wood. The thunderous retort of the gun blasted out the glass windows, and the shells shattered the old wood of the door.

"Buddy! Let's go!!!" Johnny shouted.

Buddy was still standing above his victim. The end of his nunchaku was bloody, and hair from the black man's skull was sticking to the wood. The smell of urine and excrement filled the air, giving testimony to the fact that Buddy had killed again.

Johnny grabbed Buddy and they ran alongside of the house toward their car. Buddy jumped into the driver's seat, and Johnny into the passenger's. Within moments, they were screeching down Santa Barbara Avenue.

The huge bodyguard, Jonah, had waited until he had heard the two youths running down the side of the house before moving out of the kitchen. He dropped the old black man to the floor, tried to keep himself from vomiting at the massive glob of the man's brains that rested on his pants, and ran from the house toward his car, which was parked in the alley.

He saw the old Buick take off down the street and knew generally in which direction they were headed.

Buddy drove like a madman down the empty streets as Johnny watched out the back window. When he saw the high-powered Cadillac turn out of the alleyway and immediately start gaining on them, he knew that he would have to do something. There was no way the old Buick would outrun the new Caddy.

"Buddy!" Johnny shouted. "Let the fucker catch us!"

"What, you crazy, Johnny?" Buddy screamed.

"No, man, do it! Goddamn it, slow down!!!"

Finally, Buddy took his foot off the accelerator and the car lumbered to a lower speed.

Johnny meanwhile had leaned out the window, his waist resting against the door. He held his huge pistol with two hands, aiming it directly toward the approaching car. As the Caddy quickly came up to them, Johnny unloaded four rounds of booming shells into the Caddy's windshield. As soon as the last shot was fired, he threw himself back into the car. "C'mon man, jam it!!!" he screamed to Buddy.

As Buddy stomped down on the gas pedal and the old Buick slowly picked up speed, Johnny peered over the backseat and through the rear window. What he saw made him smile a cold and brutal smile.

The Cadillac was weaving madly back and forth on the street. The windshield was completely shattered. As Johnny watched, the huge black Caddy moved wildly toward the right. It continued on up the sidewalk and headed into a gas station. Hitting the gas pump head-on, the car, along with the gas station itself, burst into a towering inferno of orange flames.

They could see the flames behind them as they drove quickly toward Santa Monica. Johnny lit a cigarette and gave one to Buddy. They did not speak, because both of them were filled with so much emotion that the words did not come.

The few people who had heard the crash stood outside the danger area of the gas station and watched the spectacular fire. The first few who had arrived had listened with horror at the blood-curdling screams of the man who was obviously trapped for the brief remainder of his life inside the fiery car.

THE BOOTH AT THE Paradise Room was occupied by two men, Duke and his bodyguard Joe. There were no women, and the remainder of the club was quiet and well behaved. It was a Sunday night, and much had gone down over the weekend that did not suit Duke.

The moment the call had come from the third numbers house on the route, Duke had reacted. He hadn't really figured that Johnny would go as far as ripping off the houses, and the news came as a slight surprise. But the handsome, middle-aged black man had dealt in the unexpected all his life and he was geared to reacting quickly to the sudden moves of others.

Duke had dispatched the two bodyguards, Jonah and Stu, out to the last house on the route, giving the men enough time to set themselves up and wait for the young hoods to show up. Then they would apprehend and return them to the Paradise Room, where Duke would take his pleasure questioning them.

But the night had worn on and the men were at least an hour overdue. Something had gone wrong and Duke knew it.

"What do you think, Joe?" Duke inquired of the large black man sitting next to him. "You think we ought to check it out?"

Joe nodded. "Yeah. Somethin' ain't right, that's for sure."

"Okay," Duke said, "get the car and let's split. Bring Eddie-Bee and Jim with us. We might need 'em."

As Joe left the club to get the other two bodyguards, Duke sipped slowly on his Jack Daniels. His mind wandered back to Leslie and her sweet presence. She had been good, he thought, but not that good.

"Damn," he said aloud to no one in particular. He knew that sooner or later his fixation on young girls would get him in trouble, and now it was causing him more than he needed. It was one of the few times in Duke's life that he ever felt badly about his sexual activities.

Duke and Joe sat in the rear of the Caddy while Eddie-Bee drove and Jim rode shotgun. The drive was short and within moments the four men were walking quickly up the front steps of the numbers house.

"We better be cool, men," Duke said as they approached the front door.

The men split up, two on each side of the door, and waited. When Duke finally nodded, they all reached into their shoulder holsters and pulled out snub-nose .38s. Duke held his lightly, then used the weapon to wave the men inside.

Joe tried the doorknob and found it locked. He backed up a step and kicked the door off the hinge. With a loud crash, the door fell into the living room of the old house.

Joe led the way through the darkened room toward the light in the kitchen. The three men followed closely. Finally, Joe peered around the doorway and into the kitchen.

"Oh shit, boss!" he said with a sick feeling in the pit of his stomach.

Duke pushed by his man into the brightly lit room. The old black man named Dave lay next to the shattered rear door, his brains seeping out of the massive hole in his skull and onto the floor. The stench was sickening and Duke covered his mouth and nose with the back of his hand.

"Uhhhh...mmmmm...."

Each man heard the low-keyed moaning sound coming from the washroom located off the kitchen. Stealthily, holding his .38 at the ready, Joe moved across the kitchen and into the washroom. When he opened the door, he found the other old man who worked with Dave cowering in the corner, trembling with fear. The slightly built little black man was drenched in his own vomit—the end result of his absolute fear.

"Duke…, it's ol' Steve, man!" Joe said.

Duke pushed aside Joe and peered into the dimly lit room. The old man stared back at Duke with wide open eyes, yet he saw nothing.

"He's in shock, Joe," Duke said calmly. "Call up some more boys. "We're goin' need to clean this shit up!"

Duke stared at the catatonic old man for a second more, then walked back to the grisly scene inside the kitchen. The back door was shattered, a ring of bullets obviously having come from the backyard and in through the old wooden door. Duke walked back to the door and went into the backyard.

At first, just the fresh air without the stench of death was a relief. But as the big man stood in the night air, lighting a cigarette, he smelled something else. It was the same horrible stench, a combination of urine, excrement and dried blood. He looked about himself frantically and finally saw the lumped figure lying near the bushes at the base of the house.

"Eddie-Bee," Duke yelled back into the house.

"Yeah, Duke?" Eddie-Bee called back from the kitchen.

"Grab a flashlight or somethin'!"

In another moment, Eddie-Bee appeared with a light. Duke grabbed the flashlight and pointed the beam at the crumpled body.

"Nunchaku!" Duke said aloud.

"Huh? What you say, boss?" Eddie-Bee asked.

"Look at his skull, man. Split wide open. Only one thing I know does that to a man. Nunchaku. An' only one cat I know uses the fucker well enough.... Buddy!"

The dead bodyguard's skull was split wide open from the forehead back to the mid-section of the head. The man's hair was tinted with blood and a seeping wet slime that Duke figured could have easily been the man's brains.

From the moment he had seen Dave, Duke knew that Johnny and Buddy had been responsible. But the sight of the bodyguard's smashed skull had given him the proof that he needed. The horrible scene was all the work of two black teenagers who were just beginning their revenge.

"Shit," Duke said as he walked back into the house. "Those motherfuckers."

Joe returned from the living room, where he had made the telephone call. "I got the boys, boss."

"Little Stu's out in the back, Joe," Duke said, now regaining his cold tone as he began thinking clearly. "An' he was fucked over by the nunchaku."

"Buddy, huh?" Joe said immediately.

"Uh huh. Johnny and Buddy. An' I can tell you right now that they ain' stoppin' here. Those dudes are out for fuckin' blood, man. Just because of that bitch sister."

Joe was about to answer but stopped when he heard a car pull into the driveway. "That must be the dudes now," Joe said as he went to the front door. Within a minute, there were five more black men, all employed by Duke, standing around the small kitchen.

"Okay, men," Duke began slowly. "This is what's happenin' here. I want this fuckin' place left exactly as it is. By that I mean I want everyone left as he is. There's another dead man, you guys know him, Stu, out in the rear. Leave him, too."

Eddie-Bee looked at his boss with shock. "Why, Duke? This fuckin' place is hot!"

"That's what I was gettin' to, my man. Now, let me pull your coattails to what's comin' down. You guys clean this fuckin' place up of all evidence linkin' me to the house. I mean, you go through every fuckin' drawer, corner and even the shit bowl and collect every piece of shit that could tell the cops this place was ever a numbers operation."

Joe nodded as the understanding of what Duke wanted dawned on him. Duke paused a moment, then continued again when he saw Joe's response.

"You can dig it, 'cause we got a dead man hit out there by a nunchaku stick. Now the fuzz got themselves a good fuckin' lead, an' maybe if we're lucky they'll use it. Otherwise we'll find the little bastards first. One way or the other, we come out fine. You guys got that?"

The men nodded in unison.

"Okay, beautiful. Now, Eddie-Bee," Duke said, turning to the slightly built bodyguard, "I want you to wait till the fuckin' place is ready for the cops, then give them a call and let them know there's been a little trouble here."

"Okay, Duke, I dig where you're comin' from!"

"All right," Duke began again, "get started. Me an' Joe are goin' out for a little visit. I want this place shit-faced clean within two hours, dig?"

Duke did not wait for the answer, but walked past Joe and out through the living room. Quickly, Joe took off after him and the two men walked hurriedly toward the black Cadillac parked in front of the house.

Johnny and Buddy's apartment was easy enough for Joe to break into. The door had opened quickly after Joe had played with the lock for a moment with his pick.

Once inside, Duke and Joe rummaged through the place, looking casually through dresser drawers and underneath the beds.

"Boss," Joe said finally, holding a bureau drawer in his hands, "what the fuck we lookin' for?"

"Somethin', man," Duke replied. "Anything that might give us a lead as to where the fuckers are."

But there was nothing. After an hour of searching through the apartment, Duke decided to leave. In his angered mind, he felt some satisfaction in letting Johnny and Buddy know that they had at least gotten to their apartment. It wasn't much, but Duke had nothing else to go on.

As the long night wore on, Duke was becoming more and more bitter. It wasn't so much that the young men had taken off the numbers houses, or even that they had killed Dave and one of Duke's bodyguards. What made the man furious was his own fear.

He had seen Buddy work with the sticks, and he had seen the coldness that could creep into Johnny's dark eyes. He knew the two youths were a powerful team when he had first seen them, that being the reason he had given them jobs. And now they were against him, and the thought made Duke shudder.

It had been some time since he had felt fear over any man, and feeling it now because of two teenagers was almost too much to handle. The Duke decided as he climbed into the Cadillac with Joe that he was going to have to do something drastic.

"Let's go to Gloria's, Joe," Duke said coldly to his driver. Joe nodded and did not try to question his boss. He could tell that Duke was preoccupied, and Joe had seen the mood before. Normally, when the Duke was in this kind of mood, someone ended up very dead.

Joe pulled up into the driveway of Gloria's house and left the motor running. He knew that Duke wasn't going inside for fun so it wouldn't take too long.

"Be right back, my man," Duke said as he climbed out of the car. He walked quickly up the stairs and onto the porch. Without knocking, he entered the house.

Gloria was just coming out of the parlor when she saw Duke. She stopped short, surprise written across her face at his unexpected presence. "Duke, what you doin' here?"

"Where's Leslie?" Duke demanded.

"Uh…, man, she's upstairs…."

"What room, Gloria?"

"Six, Duke. She's in six."

Duke walked quickly past Gloria and started upstairs. Before reaching the top, he stopped and faced her. "You got a nice load of stuff, Gloria?"

"Sure, Duke. You know I always do."

"I mean uncut, Gloria. Me an' Leslie goin' away for a while an' I wanna carry some pure shit with me. Can you do it?"

Disappointment showed itself on Gloria's face. It always did when Duke came for one of the girls. The middle-aged black woman always hoped that the man would someday come for her. "I can do it, Duke," she said finally.

"Get it ready; I'll be back in a second!"

Duke raced up the stairs and turned left down the plush hallway to room number six. He stopped outside the door and listened for a moment. He heard nothing. He tried the doorknob and found it unlocked. Taking a deep breath, he turned the knob and barged into the room.

"Jesus, fuck!!!" the nude man yelled when he saw Duke barge into the room.

"Leslie!" Duke yelled. The girl had her mouth on the man's cock and was involved in sucking him off. Her back was to the door, but when Duke yelled her name, she pulled off immediately.

"Duke!" Leslie exclaimed excitedly.

"Get dressed, babe. You an' me goin' for a little trip!" Duke had managed to control his voice now—to make it sound cool and calm.

Leslie tried to cover herself, then finally lost all sense of false modesty and ran to her closet and began

tearing out her clothes. As she dressed, the white man
sat sprawled on the edge of the bed. His passion had
dwindled to a bare memory, and as much as he wanted to speak, the fear had gripped him tightly. Duke
stood across the room and glared at the white man
with a look that melted whatever courage the man
could have ever come up with.

"C'mon, Leslie; we got to make it!" Duke said
hotly.

Finally, the young black girl was dressed, hushed
with excitement and feeling the elation that comes
when suddenly taken out of a disastrous environment.
It was much the same feeling the girl had had when
it rained at school.

Duke pushed the excited girl through the door and,
before leaving himself, turned back to the white man.
"Don't sweat, man. Gloria'll fix you up. You'll get it
off!"

Duke laughed sardonically as he closed the door
behind him. It was the kind of laugh that sent chills
through the white trick's body.

"You all ready to step out, eh?" Gloria asked as
Leslie and Duke descended the stairs. There was a
touch of bitterness in her voice, something that normally would not have bothered Duke.

"Shut up, you bitch! Ain't none of your fuckin'
business what we doin'!"

Gloria was shocked by his tone and stepped back
against the wall. In her left hand she held a little
leather packet and offered the stuff to Duke.

"All there?" he asked coldly as he snatched it,.

"Yeah, Duke. Everythin' you asked for...." Now there was a touch of fear in her voice.

"Thanks!" Duke said curtly as he led Leslie out through the front door and down the driveway. As Joe was driving the couple away from the house, Leslie began an incessant strain of chatter. She was like an excited little girl, so happy to be stepping out with the man she loved.

As her high-pitched voiced worked in his ear, Duke sat against his seat and thought. He wished the night was over because he did not like the prospect of what he was going to do. But it was something that had to be done because, if Johnny ever discovered where Leslie was working, the kid would come on strong. He would frighten away the white honkies from the establishment for a long time to come. And that would be very bad for business.

"Duke," Leslie continued—she hadn't stopped talking since leaving Gloria's—"where we goin'? We goin' for dinner, Duke? Please, I'm hungry...."

Duke glanced at the beautiful young teenager and felt his stomach tighten. It would have to be done. The source of his troubles would have to be eliminated. Everything connected with the Washington family would have to be eliminated.

"Huh?" Leslie begged. "Where we goin', Duke?"

The man sighed, then answered loud enough so that Joe in the front seat would be able to hear. "Baby, we're goin' to the Biltmore Hotel!"

Duke did not respond when the teenage girl kissed him happily on the cheek.

Duke walked hand in hand with Leslie through the lobby of the Biltmore Hotel. A few out-of-town conventioneers, some badly dressed white men off the street and a few whores lined the garishly lit lobby. The old hotel had seen better days, having once been the finest in Los Angeles. It had become in recent years a mecca for those who didn't know where to stay when visiting the city.

"I'll take a room for my daughter here an' me," Duke said to the short white man standing behind the counter. The hotelkeeper looked first at Duke, then down at Leslie. The teenage black girl looked to be anything but Duke's daughter. Her lips were slightly parted, and she was breathing hard. The white man returned his gaze to Duke.

"I'm not sure, sir. Could I see some identification, please?"

For a quick moment, Duke felt like reaching across the counter and taking the little man by the throat. Instantly, he thought better of it. He didn't want anything to happen, at least for the time being.

"Well, my man," Duke whispered in a conspiratorial tone, "you an' me, we men of the world. You dig where I'm comin' from?"

There was something about the tone of Duke's voice that put the little clerk on his guard. He nodded agreeably.

"So, I got me this little thing here…, you dig? An' I feel pretty lucky, so I'm goin' share a little bit with you in the hopes that maybe you can get yourself some later on." With that, Duke reached into his breast pocket and pulled out his wallet. The little clerk followed the progression of ten-dollar bills from Duke's billfold and into his own hands.

"Now," Duke continued, "anytime anyone comes itchin' around here askin' 'bout this little piece, you say nothin'."

"Sure," the clerk whined, taking the money, "no problem, sir."

"If there is," Duke added coldly, "you not only a poor man but you a dead man. Dig?"

The clerk tried to smile. But obviously it had been some time, if ever, that he had heard a voice as cold and menacing as Duke's. He just stood there, barely peeking over the counter, smiling and nodding like an idiot. Duke reached across and patted the man's balding pate, then laughed.

"C'mon, Leslie, let's get to our room."

"My Gawd, Duke! I ain't never seen nothin' like this!" she exclaimed, jumping onto the bed and laughing.

"It's all yours, baby," Duke said, "all yours forever."

"It's better than anythin' I ever thought I would see!"

Duke stood at the foot of the bed. He put his hand into his coat pocket and felt the small packet of heroin that Gloria had given to him earlier. He watched his beautiful little black girl laughing and playing on the bed. Not once did he feel a sense of loss or remorse. What he would do he would have to do; there was no question about it. She had brought the situation upon herself by having a brother like Johnny Washington.

Duke started to take the packet out of his pocket but was stopped midway by Leslie.

She was lying on the bed, slowly unbuttoning her blouse. Her eyes were wide with hunger, and her flesh seemed on fire.

"What you doin', Leslie?" Duke asked.

"What do you think? We didn't come up here to look at the fuckin' walls, did we?" Leslie grinned broadly, then pulled her blouse apart. Beneath, her breasts were visible—dark, rounded mounds of firm flesh capped with rich, pink nipples.

Duke attempted to halt the stirring below his belt but found the slow striptease impossible to ignore. He stood dumbfounded as Leslie pulled off her blouse. Then she began on her miniskirt. She raised her small, firm hips off the bed and slid the garment down over her legs. Her luxurious young body was revealed as she slid her panties off. Now she lay nude on the bed, her hips raised slightly off the bed. Her small, black patch shone beneath the harsh light and beckoned to Duke.

"Oh, baby…, I love you!" Leslie spread herself and beckoned to him with her arms.

Within a minute, Duke was thrusting his manhood deep inside her. He felt her body melt beneath his as she accepted all of him between her widespread thighs.

"Oh, Duke…, please…, love me, Duke, love me!"

Her sobs and moans were like those of a small animal as Duke plunged forcefully inside. She was shaking, crying and writhing beneath him, now unable to control her own movements.

Duke orgasmed, and felt Leslie shudder, then raise herself off the bed and collapse. She held him tightly between her thighs. "I never want you to leave, Duke. Never!" she moaned.

"Baby," Duke replied, his mind drifting back to the business at hand, "I'll never leave you again. As long as you're alive."

Leslie smiled trustingly up at the big man above her. She thought she saw love and kindness in his dark brown eyes. But her own were so clouded with the mist of love that she missed the cold brutality that existed there. "You mean that, Duke?"

"Sure, baby, sure," Duke replied as he lifted himself from between her legs. He walked across the room and pulled out a cigarette from his coat pocket. Lighting it, he regarded Leslie's nude body once again.

"Duke," Leslie said, "come on over here. I'll do something real special...."

The thought crossed his mind again, his loins began to speak. But then his brain cut in, and he knew there would be no more partaking of her fine young body. At least, Duke thought, I'll be the last man she ever has.

"Duke?" Leslie called again.

The man smiled at Leslie, then reached inside his coat pocket and pulled out the packet of white powder. He showed the stuff to Leslie.

"Oh no, Duke," she said. "We don' need that shit. Not tonight...."

"Ah, baby," Duke said, grabbing Leslie's purse and pulling out her spoon and hypo. "We gonna do it right. I mean, you think it was good last time, jus' wait till you see what happens after a little of this shit!"

"But Duke," the teenager protested, "I don't really need it now. I mean, I got you here an' that's all I ever needed."

"C'mon, baby, do it for Duke. I wanna see you really get off."

She watched the man helplessly from the bed as he prepared her stuff. He functioned with a timeless expertise, measuring out the proper amount, heating it just right and sterilizing the needle. Leslie had learned the art well, but she was no match for Duke. His fingers were nimble and he was quick. Leslie had never thought of Duke as a user, but now she wondered.

"Duke?" she began.

"Yeah, baby?"

"You ever..., you know, use?"

Duke laughed out loud. He turned toward her with the hypo in his hand. A smile worked its way across his face. "Sure, baby," he said, "as a matter of fact, as soon as you finish with your shit, I'm goin' to make myself a little taste."

Leslie was disappointed and she was relieved. She didn't want it by herself and would have liked to have Duke with her. The fact that he had offered to shoot up after she had finished relaxed her and made the needle much easier to accept.

"I'm glad," Leslie said as she took the hypo from Duke. "'Cause we goin' have one kind of night tonight."

"We sure are, baby. We sure are...."

Duke stood above her and watched her as she took the needle and directed it into her already well-used vein. Expertly, the young, naked teenager pushed the needle deep into herself, then pushed the mixture of uncut heroin into her lifestream.

"Ah..., Jesus...," Leslie moaned when she had emptied the tube of its contents.

"Feel good, baby?" Duke asked, waiting.

"Yeah..., Jesus...."

He watched her closely. Her eyes rolled back into her head. Her naked flesh took on an unnatural sheen. She reached down and grasped the sides of the bed, then began flinching, struggling as if out of oxygen.

Duke knew that it would be a matter of only a few more moments. The sight of her naked body, writhing and twisting beneath the force of the overdose, excited him. He stood above her, still naked, and found that he was erect again.

Leslie began shuddering horribly, her nervous system jumping and shorting out as the heroin surged through her body. A trickle of urine poured from between her legs, and her bowels emptied onto the bed. Her twitching then increased violently and then just as quickly stopped.

Duke found himself dismayed by the horrible scene

before him. The stench in the room was suffocating. Her body had emptied itself, and even though her naked flesh was sprawled across the bed, she became in his eyes the most undesirable woman he had ever seen.

Quickly he dressed. Then he went around the room and wiped every piece of furniture with a handkerchief. He made sure that Leslie's needle was in plain view. Feeling the adrenalin surging through his body as he did at the moment of death, he walked from the room and out into the hall.

The stairway to the rear of the building was cold and empty. Duke took it two steps at a time. The smell of death was still on him, and it seemed that, no matter how quickly he ran, he could not shake it.

Joe was waiting in the alley behind the hotel with the Cadillac. Duke climbed into the backseat and sighed.

"Everythin' all right, Duke?" Joe asked, seeing the condition that Duke was in.

"Yeah, my man, nothin' bad comin' down. Nothin' that a little Jack Daniels and one of Gloria's broads couldn't make well again."

Joe chuckled as he pulled onto Fifth Street and headed toward Wilshire. The evening traffic was ebbing, and the streets were virtually empty. Joe drove until he hit a liquor store. He parked in front, disappeared inside for a moment, then returned with a quart of Jack Daniels.

"Beautiful, my man. Beautiful!" Duke took the bottle, unscrewed the cap and drained off a good amount of the whiskey. After he had taken another couple of slugs, he passed the bottle back to Joe.

"Yeah!" Joe exclaimed after his belt, "that stuff sure has the power of gold!"

Duke laughed, feeling the warming effect drive through him. Already, his head was beginning to clear. He was turning back into his old self again and regaining control.

"Hey," Duke called out, "let's make it on over to Gloria's and have a taste of another sort!"

"I dig where you're comin' from!" Joe exclaimed happily. The big man was always relieved when Duke was able to pull himself out of one of his moods. Joe lived for Duke, and the boss's passions and upsets were his, too. When Duke was down, then so was Joe. And when Duke was up, Joe always went along for the ride.

The moment Gloria saw Duke, she knew that Leslie was dead. Duke knew that she knew; he could see it in her eyes. But Gloria was too afraid to say anything. Instead, she just looked at the big man coldly and tried to smile.

"Gloria," Duke began, "I need a little relaxation, you dig?"

"Which one you want, Duke?" Gloria asked.

"Young stuff..., you got some young stuff?"

"Sure, baby. We always got young stuff..., you know that."

Duke waited for a moment while Gloria ran up the stairs calling out the name Pat. Finally, she appeared with a very young black girl, a thin, scrawny girl who had barely had time to fill out properly before being called into Duke's service.

"Duke, honey," Gloria began, pushing Pat out in front of her, "this here's Pat. One of our finest and one of our youngest."

Pat tried to smile, but the corners of her mouth quivered. She was nervous and afraid.

Duke walked up the stairs and right past the young black girl. "Bring her to the bath...."

Gloria led Pat down the hall and into the bathroom where Duke had two years ago installed a large Japanese tub. Gloria leaned down and started the water. "Honey," she yelled over her shoulder, "you best rid yourself of those clothes. The man likes 'em naked and hot!"

The young girl quickly disrobed. She stood naked in the center of the room. Her thin body looked even more emaciated than before. Her breasts were barely developed. The richness that a woman possesses in her body was nowhere evident. Skin and bones was all that the young girl had to offer a man.

Duke entered the bathroom wearing his silken robe which he kept on the premises. Gloria walked over to him and pulled the expensive cloth from his body. The large black man stepped naked into the tub and waited for Pat.

"Go ahead, Pat, he's all yours...." Gloria looked once to Duke, then left the room.

Pat bent down and began washing Duke. She tried her best to look sexy, to act the role of the experienced woman. But her body betrayed her.

Duke looked at the young girl for the first time. He was shocked by her youth, something that he had not confronted in all his years of hustling young girls. She was like some kind of foreign being to him. It seemed impossible that he would become aroused by her presence.

"Is everythin' all right, Mr. Duke?" Pat asked in a trembling voice.

Duke felt himself lose control. "Get the fuck outta here!" he screamed.

Pat bolted from the room, slamming the door behind her. Gloria was inside the bathroom immediately.

"Duke!" Gloria shouted when she saw the rage that filled him.

"Where'd you get that little bitch?" he demanded.

"You, Duke..., you brought her here...."

"Shit, Gloria, no way! I would've never touched somethin' like her!" Duke felt himself tense, then felt his body begin to tremble.

"C'mon, baby, you best get out of that tub!" Gloria could see it coming. She knew that what had happened with Leslie was affecting him. Duke had killed a lot of men in his time and had driven a lot of innocent young girls into drugs and prostitution. But in all the years that she had known him, Duke had never murdered as he had that night.

"Listen, baby," Gloria began after she had taken Duke back to her bedroom and made him lie on her bed, "you got a killin' on your mind, an' you're gonna get fucked up if you don't watch out."

"Shut up, woman!" Duke yelled. "Ain't none of your damn business what goes down outside this house!"

Gloria took a deep breath. What she was about to say was something she would have never even dreamed a week ago. She felt her body tense and her adrenalin begin to flow. "Duke," she began softly, "you took that little girl out of here tonight and you came back without her. The way I see it, you didn't drop her off at no bus station and tell her to leave Los Angeles. I mean, you wouldn't risk none of that shit...."

"What are you tryin' to say?" Duke demanded.

"I'm sayin' what I said before, Duke. You got a killin'..., you murdered Leslie!"

There was a long pause. Duke stared at the woman hard. His eyes seemed to dig into her soul, but she would not turn away. This time, Gloria thought, this time I'll beat him and free myself.

But Duke was too strong. Gloria had conjured up the one emotion that was Duke's strongest weapon—his hatred. She had challenged him, and he had responded. Had she been a man, she would have been lying stone dead on the floor. But since she was a woman, she would be made love to by Duke.

It was all over in a few moments, and Gloria lay trembling beneath Duke. She kept calling him her man.

Duke lifted himself above the woman and gently stroked her cheek. "Everythin' all right now, baby?"

he asked soothingly.

Gloria looked up into his cold, chiseled face. A voice that did not seem her own answered with a soft yes. In her mind, Gloria knew that Leslie was now gone. She would be mentioned no more.

12

THE SUN WAS RISING in the east on a cloudy, cold Monday morning. Policemen, the coroner and reporters were milling inside the old numbers house. A few men were in the backyard, staring down at the sheet-draped body of Duke's former bodyguard. The men's voices were muffled in the early morning heaviness.

Detective Jim Spence stood above the body of the dead man in the backyard. He had already seen the mutilated body of the old man inside the kitchen and there was nothing abnormal about the killing. The usual gunshot and the usual after-effects of a bullet blowing apart a man's skull. But out here, in the backyard, things were different.

"Tom?" Spence yelled into the kitchen. "Come on out here!"

Detective Tom Baker pushed his way through the crowded kitchen and out the back door. He walked up to the side of his black partner and stopped.

"Tom, you seen this one yet?"

"No. Haven't got a chance to." Baker watched as his partner kneeled down and pulled back the sheet from the corpse.

"Jesus!" Baker exclaimed when the sight of the man's smashed skull hit him. It was the same feeling of revulsion and unexplained fear that he had had that morning weeks ago at the railroad yards when he had seen the security guard. That man's head had been split open in the same manner as this black man's.

"Nunchaku?" Baker asked.

Spence nodded, then pulled the sheet back over the dead man's head. The detective turned to the county coroner, who was waiting patiently nearby. "Okay, you can take him away."

The coroner nodded, called out to his associate and began lifting the corpse onto a stretcher. Newsmen were snapping their cameras as the body was wheeled around the side of the house and out toward the wagon.

Jim Spence walked slowly to the other side of the yard, lit a cigarette and turned back to survey the rear of the house. The fingerprint specialists, along with uniformed policemen, were inside searching the premises for clues. So far nothing had shown up.

"What do you make of it?" Detective Baker asked his partner after joining him near the fence.

"There's no doubt, Tom. It was a nunchaku. The clean hit, the force of the blow, everything about the wound indicates it was the same weapon used out at the yards."

"Okay, then," Tom began slowly, "we got a house with an old man shot inside. Another, much younger man bearing a weapon is killed outside with the nunchaku. Probably by the same person who knocked off the security guard. So where does that leave us?"

"Not much better off than before," Spence replied, drawing heavily on his cigarette. "But there's got to be some reason for all this. If the lab boys can come up with something about this house, what, if any, operation was taking place inside, we might be on our way."

"Numbers, I'd say offhand," Baker added.

"No doubt, if there was anything at all." Spence moved away from the fence and began walking back toward the rear of the house. He was ponderous, and as his white partner followed, he began thinking out loud.

"Tom," he began in a quiet voice, "if it was the same two boys who killed the guard, then something has happened to them in the last couple of weeks."

"How do you mean that, Jim?" Baker listened intently. It was during moments like these that his black partner seemed to gain tremendous insight into the workings of whomever they were after.

"Well," Spence continued, stopping in the middle

of the lawn and facing his partner, "at the rail yards we had what looked like a possible self-defense, right?"

"Yes. Almost had to be."

"Okay," Spence continued, "a couple of kids looting a boxcar is something quite different from cold-blooded murder. This scene here just looks like a rip-off, and cold-blooded murder thrown in. Somewhere between the incident at the yards and last night, the Washington kid and his friend went through some mighty heavy changes. You agree?"

Baker was silent for a moment, then sighed. "Yeah, I can see your point, Jim. But we don't know for sure that they weren't killers to begin with. Maybe you're trying to tie them in with something more."

"Uh huh, that's right," Spence replied, his eyes cold and determined. "I just have the feeling these little fish are swimming in bigger waters now."

Before Baker could add anything, a young, white policeman approached the two detectives. In his right hand he held a piece of paper.

"Sir," the uniformed officer began, "I found this slip inside the toilet bowl. It looked like someone had tried to flush it down, but it got backed up."

Spence took the slip and read the blurred, water-soaked writing. What he saw made his heart jump. It was a numbers slip with an account and the beginning of a man's name.

"What is it, Jim?" Baker asked.

"Numbers. You were right, Tom. The house was a numbers house."

The white officer beamed. "We've searched everywhere inside, sir, and it appears that the whole place has been cleaned out."

"That's okay, officer," Spence said, "this is enough for right now. Good work!"

"All right," Baker said, "we got them knocking off a numbers house. So what?"

"Numbers operations have operators, Tom," Spence began. "We find out who runs it down here, in this part of town, and we get inside and follow the man. Because two kids like we're after can't knock off a house, kill two of the men, and expect to just walk away. Whoever runs this piece of action is going to come after those boys with everything he's got."

"And," Baker added, now seeing the direction of his partner's thoughts, "if we manage to get close, we'll get both of 'em!"

"Exactly, Tom. We got ourselves a break here that could lead us right into the center of the volcano."

The two detectives started walking back into the house when another officer called out to them that there was a call for them on the radio. Spence jogged around the side of the house and out to the front, where his car was parked.

The neighbors had gathered, and a silent, hushed crowd of onlookers, mostly black, stood in the early morning chill like a disappointed audience at a sporting event.

"Spence here...," the detective said as he leaned into his car. Detective Harmon Mason, a longtime friend and associate, talked excitedly over the radio.

"Jim," Mason began, "we got a possible suicide, possible homicide over here at the Biltmore Hotel. Either way, it's an overdose. She's a young kid, appears to have just started with the poison."

"Why call me?" Spence asked.

"Well," Mason continued, "I know you guys were on the Washington case, you know, the security guard killing? The kid's name here is Washington, Jim. Leslie Marie Washington, and her home address is the same as Johnny Washington's. Jim, the dead girl is your fugitive's sister!"

"Damn, Harmon, we'll be right over! Stall the coroner's people till we get there!"

"Okay, Jim. I'll keep 'em off."

Jim Spence replaced the receiver, jumped into the driver's seat and started the engine. His mind was racing fast now. Something was coming down out there, and he had to get to it before it exploded. The pieces were all starting to fall into place, but the links were still missing.

Detective Baker ran to the car and jumped in beside his partner after hearing Spence blasting the horn. The two men raced away from the scene of the murder toward the scene of another.

Her body was sprawled across the large double bed in the room on the eleventh floor. Detective Harmon Mason, a heavy, middle-aged white man, pulled back the sheet and revealed the splendid nude body of Leslie Washington to Detectives Spence and Baker. The smell of urine and excrement was strong in the room, and the sheets of the bed were soiled beneath the young girl's body.

"Leslie Washington," Mason said simply.

"Okay, Harmon," Spence said, feeling a definite rage seep through his veins. On the drive over to the hotel, he had excitedly discussed the possibilities that the death of Johnny Washington's sister would have on the case. But now, after seeing the young, beautiful black girl soiled and dirty on the bed, the excitement turned to pure revulsion and anger.

"Shit, she was young!" Baker said.

"Yeah, according to the work permit we found in her purse, she was only fifteen," Mason added.

Detective Mason nodded to the waiting coroner, then took Spence and Baker into the adjoining sitting room of the hotel suite. There the three men lit cigarettes.

"We checked with the doorman and the bellhop downstairs, and also with the desk," Mason began, "and we found out she came in with an older black man around two-thirty this morning. The guy at the desk said the man paid with cash and signed under the name Bill Smith. He said the dude looked like he had money and that the girl, Leslie, looked happy and excited."

"Have you checked the smack?" Spence asked Mason.

"Yeah. Pure, uncut. There were some particles in the bathroom. She did it to herself, we think."

"But," Baker added, "she didn't know what she was taking, right?"

"Yup, that's why it's not a definite suicide. And the guy who brought her in…." Mason's voice trailed off.

"The guy who brought her in, Tom," Spence began, "has something to do with Washington. There's too much coincidence here. Way too much!"

"I agree, Jim," Baker said, "but we don't have the connection, yet."

Spence drew on his cigarette and moved his large frame off the dresser he had been leaning against. His mind worked feverishly; everything was falling in front of him, but still there was no connection. Finally, he reached the point where they had begun. "That fuckin' little fence, you remember him, Tom?"

Baker thought for a moment. "Yeah, Sam?"

"Right. We still got him?"

"Nope," Baker replied. "Had to let him out. Couldn't hold him more than three days. He made his bail."

"Okay, let's pick him up," Spence said sharply. "An older black man who travels with fifteen-year-old girls got to have somethin' happening for himself. And a man with that kind of perversity shouldn't be too difficult to find. Sam'll know who the bastard is!"

"You sure, Jim? The little prick's frightened; you remember that!"

"Shit," Spence said, his words coming fast and strong now, "we'll get it out of him."

The way he said it frightened Baker. When Spence was determined and smelled a solution, there were very few obstacles that he would let get in his way. Needless to say, a hustling fence wasn't one of them.

As Spence and Baker started out of the room, now devoid of the body of Leslie Washington, Detective Mason stopped them. "Who's going to tell the parents?" Mason asked, knowing that Spence would feel obligated because of his color to tell the girl's folks.

Spence looked at Mason, then at the floor. "I'm grateful to you, Harmon, for bringing us in on this. But could you do it? I've done it once so far on this case, and right now I don't think we have the time."

Detective Mason smiled. He knew he shouldn't have taken advantage of Spence's color. "Okay, Jim. Sorry I asked."

"No reason to be sorry, Harmon," Spence replied with a cold, cynical smile. "I was the logical choice."

Mason chuckled and turned back into the hotel room. Spence and Baker headed down to their car, and as soon as they were inside they issued an A.P.B. for the little black man called Sam.

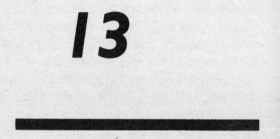

13

LATE IN THE AFTERNOON, the fog moved in off the Pacific Ocean and virtually encased the Venice area in its murky presence. The little house on the canal was shrouded in the moist gray matter, and the stillness of the neighborhood was oppressive.

Johnny Washington sat alone inside the living room next to the telephone. Anita's grandmother was in the kitchen preparing the dinner, which would consist of a potato pie, black-eyed peas and a chocolate cake for dessert. But the fine smells emanating from the kitchen went unnoticed by the stunned young black man.

It had taken one phone call by Johnny to set his

mind in a direction that he knew he would follow through to the end. Whatever doubts he had had about doing justice to Duke were now a thing of the past. Leslie was dead. She had been found in a hotel room with an overdose of heroin in her veins. His little sister was the one person besides Anita who had meant something in the way of motivation to him.

Everything he and Buddy had done had been done for them, and now one of them was dead. The shock of hearing his mother tell him that his little sister was dead had still not worn itself off. The only thoughts working through the young black's mind were those of death. If it was the last thing he would ever do on the face of the earth, he would kill Duke.

Johnny knew that there was nothing else left to do. Tonight, with or without Buddy, he would have to put a bullet through the bastard's skull!

"Hey, Johnny, what's happenin'?" Buddy walked in from the outside where he and Anita and Jane had been strolling up and down the boardwalk.

"Leslie's dead, Buddy," Johnny said blankly.

"What, man?"

"She's dead. Duke...killed her."

Buddy looked at his friend and saw the cold, stark hatred that filled Johnny's eyes. He knew instantly that there was going to be a price to pay. "Shit...," Buddy said, now feeling the shock move through his mind.

Johnny looked up at his friend for the first time. He stood up and faced Buddy. "I'm going to kill Duke, Buddy. I'm goin' blow his fuckin' brains out!"

Buddy just nodded. There was little he could say to a statement of purpose like that.

"You don't have to come with me, Buddy," Johnny said, his voice still flat and cold. "You been a good friend, man. An' I appreciate everything you've done. But you don't have to come with me. You can take our money and the girls and make it to Frisco. You dig where I'm comin' from?"

"I dig it, Johnny," Buddy said, feeling the icy hatred beginning to capture his own mind. "But we been through a lot of shit together. Leslie was like a sister to me, too. I'm with you all the way, Johnny."

Johnny was moved by Buddy's loyalty. "Thank you, man."

At that moment, Anita and Jane entered the house, laughing and squealing like little girls. Johnny had never seen his girlfriend happier than she had been during the short time they had spent at the beach. The dark dread that Johnny had known and felt was now a complete reality, but he also knew that he would have to do everything possible to keep it from Anita. He couldn't let her know what was happening.

"Hey, Anita," Johnny said, trying to sound light and cheerful. "We takin' a trip!"

"A trip? Where?" Anita's eyes opened wide.

"Frisco, baby. You an' Jane goin' up right now, soon as you can pack. Me an' Buddy got some business to take care of, then we'll join you later tonight."

"How come, Johnny? Why don't we just wait for you till then?" Anita asked.

"No questions, baby. You an' Jane get yourselves

together. Okay?"

Anita looked from Johnny to Buddy, then back to Buddy again. She had begun to learn that certain questions should not be asked. She could tell by the look on Buddy's face that this was one of those times. "Okay, Johnny, we'll pack."

Johnny and Buddy said their goodbyes to the old woman, shocking her because they were leaving so soon. The grandmother had become heartened with the young people's presence and had gone out of her way to make everything as fine as possible during their visit.

Johnny was saddened by the look of disappointment on the woman's wrinkled black face when he told her they would have to leave. The old woman's loneliness had been temporarily forgotten. But now it was returning again and she could not hide her feelings.

The two couples then drove in silence to L.A. International Airport. The gloomy day was now turning into night, and the line of rush-hour traffic heading out of the city made their voyage lengthy.

Finally, Johnny pulled Anita's old Buick into the airport parking lot. Each girl had a suitcase, and Johnny and Buddy carried them into the terminal.

They had a half hour before the plane took off. Johnny and Anita sat in the waiting area while Buddy and Jane walked throughout the terminal. Being in an airport for the first time, they were fascinated by the modern, glass-enclosed building.

"Johnny," Anita began softly, "you got to tell me

what's goin' on. I know something is."

Johnny squirmed in his seat. He had known this would be coming from Anita and had hoped the plane would depart right away in order to avoid it. "Nothin', babe. Nothin's happenin'. Me an' Buddy just got some shit to take care of. We'll be up later tonight."

She looked at him closely. On the way to the airport, Anita had watched his lean black face closely. He had not said a word in the car, and many times during the ride it appeared as though he was ready to break out in tears. Anita was worried, but she knew that she could not press him too hard.

"I'm sorry, honey," Anita said, putting her arms around Johnny's neck. "I didn't mean to pry or anything like that. I just have this feelin', you know?"

"No sense to that, Anita," Johnny replied. "We're goin' be all right. Isn't that what I've been telling you all along? You just got to trust me, that's all."

Anita leaned over and buried her face in his shoulder. She was afraid, really afraid this time, and it was getting difficult for her to conceal the fear she had. The previous Saturday night, when both Johnny and Buddy had returned with their bruises, had frightened her, but she had been around the streets long enough not to have been too shocked.

But this sudden departure, and the urgency and quietness of Johnny, had been something that she had never confronted before. And it frightened her terribly.

Buddy and Jane returned from their tour of the airport. Jane was in high spirits. She had not known

Buddy long enough to realize that something important was happening. "We saw a 747!" Jane exclaimed in her excited, high-pitched voice.

"Yeah," Buddy added. "Some monster motherfucker!"

"We gonna fly in one?" Jane asked.

"No way," Buddy replied. "You'll take a smaller one. It's only an hour's flight time up there. No need to use the big planes."

And the conversation turned to airplanes. None of them had ever flown before, and Johnny was happy to see the excitement in Anita as she began realizing that she was going to take her first flight. At least it was a hell of a lot better than dwelling on their separation.

"Flight 852 to San Francisco now boarding at gate forty-seven," the booming voice said over the public address system.

"That's you, baby," Johnny said, getting to his feet.

"I just can't believe we're going! This is too much!" Jane was practically drunk with excitement. She pulled Buddy by the hand across the waiting room and to the boarding gate. Johnny and Anita walked arm in arm behind, at a much slower pace.

"Listen," Johnny began when they approached the boarding turnstile, "you get a room at the Regency Hotel downtown. I saw an ad for it in a magazine once and it looks like a fine place."

"Okay," Anita said, staring at the floor.

"Listen, we'll be there tonight sometime. Then we'll all go out an' have some fine kind of dinner.

They got seafood up there that's outta sight, from what I hear!"

Anita still stared at the floor. Finally, she looked up and there were tears in her eyes. She threw her arms around Johnny and kissed him long and passionately.

"C'mon, Anita," Jane yelled, already inside the boarding area, "this ain't no time for that kind of thing!"

Buddy and Jane laughed.

Finally, Anita broke away from Johnny and presented her ticket to the well-dressed clerk, then made her way with Jane down the carpeted tunnel and into the body of the airplane parked outside the terminal. Buddy and Johnny stood and watched them disappear around the corner.

"Well," Buddy said, "that's that!"

"No, man. We'll catch them later tonight." But Johnny's voice did not hold the conviction he tried to muster with his words. Buddy looked at him and felt his own adrenalin pouring through his body. He reached beneath his coat and felt the comforting hardness of his nunchaku sticks. It was going to be a long, cold night.

As the two black youths worked their way through the heavy airport traffic, two much older men were attempting to work their way through the fears and stubbornness of a plump, balding black man.

In the interrogation room of the South Central police station, Sam the fence was beginning to feel as though his life had been doomed by the two detec-

tives who stood angrily over him. The harsh light from
the bulb blinded him, and already the sweat was trick-
ling down his flabby body.

The questions had been coming at him for most of
the afternoon, and he hadn't told the two policemen
what they wanted to know. Earlier in the afternoon,
Sam had been picked up near his apartment and
brought directly to the police building. No charges had
been made and Sam had known that the arrest had
been an illegal one.

Yet there had been nothing he could do about it.
Detectives Spence and Baker had wanted information,
and they wanted it fast. Legal matters had obviously
been too time-consuming to even consider.

Detective Spence leaned against the wall, dumped
his cigarette on the bare wood floor and ground it out
slowly with the heel of his shoe. "Now then, my
friend," he began coldly, "tell us again what you know
about the operation of certain big-time dudes in
Watts."

Sam squirmed in his chair. The same question had
been coming at him for what seemed like an eterni-
ty.

Jim Spence glared at the little black man. His mind
traveled back in time to that first night when he and
Tom had gotten the names of Johnny Washington and
Buddy out of the frightened little fence. At that time,
the names had belonged to two young punks who had
killed a security guard at the yards. This time, the
name they were after could very well be a big one,
and Spence was preparing himself to go as far as nec-

essary to get that name. He could taste it, he could smell it, and he wasn't about to let it slip through his fingers.

"Now, come on," Detective Baker began before Spence could continue, "all we want is a name. Some dude down here who digs the young broads..., like thirteen, fifteen years old. You dig it, Sam?"

"I tol' you guys," Sam whined, "I don't know of anyone like that...."

"Like shit you don't!" Spence bellowed. "You know every fuckin' piece of action that's goin' down in Watts! So you better open that mouth of yours and utter somethin' we can use!"

Sam lowered his head and stared at his tightly clenched hands. He was going to try and make it through. He felt confident that the detectives, especially the black one, wouldn't get too violent with him. All he had gotten last time was a threat and a slap across the face. After that interrogation, the little man had gotten down on himself for breaking so soon.

Sam had always wanted to make it big, and he figured now if he could just hang on and get out, he would be able to go to the Duke and warn him. That, Sam figured, would certainly guarantee him a prime spot in the big man's future plans.

"Sam," Spence began again, his voice icy cold and soft, "we know there's a cat down there doin' numbers, sellin' smack and runnin' little girls into prostitution. It's the same fuckin' game played in every damn ghetto throughout the country. We got a chance to break it here, and we need your help. We got a murder one against the dude so we can do it!"

Spence waited. He had made his plea hoping that some sense of decency was left in the chubby black man. But when Sam just turned his sweaty head away, Spence knew that there was nothing left that he could tap.

"One more time," Baker said. "We're giving you one more time, Sam. If you keep that trap of yours shut, we'll nail you on a conspiracy charge."

"Ain' no way you'll catch...." Sam stopped himself. He felt his stomach sicken.

"Okay, man," Spence said. "Now we know that you know the dude. You got one fuckin' minute left."

Spence moved a step closer to the sweating little man while Baker stood up and moved to Sam's other side. Both detectives stood over the man, waiting.

"Anything you want to say, my man?" Spence asked finally.

"You can't do nothin' to me," Sam said finally, with a tinge of desperation in his voice. "It's police brutality, man!"

Spence laughed sardonically. "Tom, that door locked in here?"

"Sure is, Jim," Baker replied.

Jim Spence moved closer to Sam, reached down and grabbed the smaller black man by the lapels of his coat. In one motion, Spence had Sam on his feet. He turned the frightened little man toward the corner and pushed him up against the wall.

Sam's face was pressed against the wall and Spence

started pushing him harder and harder. It felt as though all his facial bones were being crushed one against the other as Spence exerted more and more pressure. Sam tried to turn his head to the side, but it was impossible. Another second and his nose would be broken.

"C'mon, baby," Spence said coldly, "just one fuckin' little name and you might have a nose left!"

The pressure was to the point where Sam heard his own bones beginning to crack. The pain flashed through his brain, sending sheets of white light through his skull. He began to feel a wave of nausea grip his belly. Spence exerted a little more pressure.

"C'mon, bastard!" Spence said.

And then Sam let go. He felt his bladder empty. The warm urine ran down the insides of his pants leg. Then his bowels emptied and the room was filled with the sickening stench of his excrement.

"You poor little bastard!" Spence said when he realized what had happened. "It's going to get worse!"

Suddenly, Spence pulled his victim away from the wall and hurled Sam like a dummy across the room and into the opposing wall. The little black man lay crumpled and beaten on the floor, his eyes glazed and his nose twisted in a grotesque angle to the right.

"There's a dude...," Sam began, trying to hold back the tears, "in the Paradise Room. On Compton. They call him Duke...."

"What's his real name?" Baker asked excitedly.

"Don't know, man. I swear...." And then little Sam fainted, his eyes rolling back into his head as a glob of vomit poured from his mouth and nostrils.

Spence turned his back on the sight, feeling a wave of sickness run through his body. He called out to the guard and had Sam taken to the infirmary. "Get him fixed up," Spence said to the policeman, "and lock him up for his own protection."

"Should we move in with everything?" Baker asked as he and Spence walked quickly from the little room.

Spence thought for a moment before replying. "No. That place is hot as hell down there. We bring in an army and we're going to have a riot on our hands. You and me, Tom. We'll go in alone for right now."

Detectives Spence and Baker ran downstairs to the garage and jumped into their unmarked car. For the first time in a long time, Jim Spence felt as though he were about to start paying back those black brothers who had brought so much pain and misery to his people.

It was Monday night at the Paradise Room and the club was dark. Inside the main room the chairs were piled upside down on the tables, the glasses were stacked on the bar, and most of the lights were turned off. Al the bartender worked quietly behind the empty bar, washing glasses and putting the bottles of liquor in order for the upcoming week.

Joe leaned back against the table in the far corner of the room. He was dressed tonight, wearing a blue mohair suit that he saved for important occasions. Jim and Eddie-Bee, the other two bodyguards, sat at the table itself and smoked cigarettes in silence. They were all waiting for Duke.

Upstairs in his apartment, Duke was completing his shaving. He stood in front of the mirror, pulling his razor against his smooth, black skin. He was relaxed now. He had made his decision and there was nothing more to think about.

Earlier in the morning, after he had left the Biltmore Hotel, with Leslie slowly drifting toward death in the room upstairs, he had begun thinking intently about how he was going to handle the situation with Johnny and Buddy. He knew that eventually Johnny was going to find out about his sister, and when he did, Duke knew the kid was going to come after him.

At first, the man's inclination had been to stay and fight it out with Johnny, to draw the boy into his own territory and wipe him forever off the face of the earth. In the deeper recesses of Duke's mind, that had been one of the prime motivations behind giving Leslie the last overdose of heroin. That, and the clean quickness of getting rid of her forever.

The scheme of drawing Johnny and Buddy into his turf would have worked ten years ago. Duke had fought and killed to get control of the terrain he now held, and during those years he had not been afraid of any man. But with success came softness. Having men like Joe around him constantly allowed Duke to lose his hunter's instinct, to relax in his bid for survival in the concrete jungle.

That cold, calculating mind that had won so many battles had been replaced with an obsession, a need for young and pretty girls. Fortunately, Duke thought to himself, I am smart enough to realize that.

So, the big man had decided that the best way to settle the matter would be to leave the killings in the hands of men now better equipped to kill. Joe, Jim and Eddie-Bee were hungry, and they would do anything for Duke. They would lie in wait for Johnny and Buddy while Duke himself lounged in the comfort of a hotel in Las Vegas.

The tall black man wiped his face clean, poured on some expensive after-shave lotion and pulled his silken shirt off the hanger. He dressed hurriedly because he was anxious to get out. The stage had been set, and he knew that it was only a matter of time before the players were to begin coming onstage.

Duke walked into his bedroom, pulled his suitcase shut and snapped the catches. He searched around the room, looking for anything that he might have forgotten. His suede coat was lying on the circular bed, and he put that on. He grabbed up his suitcase and started for the door. Just make it to the airport, he thought, and Joe'll take care of those little bastards!

Downstairs, inside the Paradise Room, the avengers were waiting patiently for their man. Each man was dressed especially well, as though ceremoniously attempting to get themselves up for what they knew was an approaching showdown. Each man carried .357 magnums instead of their usual snub-nose .38s, and the bulges inside their jackets were unmistakable.

"We dump those rods before we go into the airport, gentlemen," Duke warned.

"Yeah, don't worry, boss," Joe replied.

Duke was anxious to leave. He had keyed himself to getting out of the place, and time was running out. But his plane was not due to take off for yet another two hours, and the man did not want to sit around the airport for an hour.

"C'mon, Al," Duke said, resting against the edge of the table next to Joe, "let's give my men here some liquid refreshment!"

Al scurried behind the bar, pulled out a half-full bottle of Jack Daniels and brought that and four glasses over to the man's table. Duke grabbed the bottle and poured large shots for each man. They raised their glasses to the center of the table in the form of a salute.

"Gentlemen," Duke said, "success in Vegas. And keep it cool here!"

They agreed in unison, and each man took a long swig from his glass.

The three bodyguards had known what was happening with Johnny and Buddy. They knew that the kid was out for blood because of his sister. But only one of the three had any suspicion at all that Leslie was dead. When Duke had finally come down from the hotel room the night before, Joe had asked him about the teenage girl.

"I tol' her to get out of this fuckin' city!" Duke had said, sliding into the backseat of the car.

But Joe had wondered about that. It wasn't like Duke to leave his girls hanging like that, no matter how much trouble they might have caused. And then,

earlier in the afternoon, the Duke had revealed his trip
to Las Vegas to the men. He had told them that he
was setting up a contact for smack in that town and
that wealth would befall them all if the deal went
through.

Joe had asked him about Johnny and Buddy. Duke
had told him that, in case they showed their faces,
they should be disposed of. "But," Duke had added
rather quickly, "I doubt the littl' bastards are still in
town. You dig? But be careful anyway, and keep on
your toes."

It had worried Joe because he had never known his
boss to run out on trouble when it came his way. And
these two young black men were definitely not light-
weights, even with their age. They were forces on the
streets to be contended with.

And yet, Duke seemed to be now taking them lightly. For a brief moment, Joe had had the incredible
thought that possibly his man was running away, using
his bodyguards to take the brunt of whatever was coming from the young dudes. But Joe had wiped the
thought away as quickly as it had come. He had been
with the Duke too long now to ever think the man
would run from a confrontation.

Now, as the men stood around drinking in the
empty club, Duke was chatting in a light-hearted,
excited manner. "An' we get that fucker set up, we
run right through Vegas and into the other Nevada
cities. We can pack the stuff with some of the girls
working the whore ranches and set up a groovy net-
work. I'll tell you guys somethin', if this fucker goes

through, we're all gonna be rich!"

"I can dig that!" Eddie-Bee said, running his hand through his large Afro at the thought of wealth.

"Yeah," Jim added, shifting his light frame on the seat, "that sounds all right, Duke."

Duke looked from one man to the other. He knew he had them behind him all the way. He knew the secret working of money and how it served to alleviate a man's doubts. Even Joe seemed to be for the idea.

"Yeah, Duke," Joe said slowly, "that sounds real fine."

The man smiled and poured another round of drinks. The soothing effect of the whiskey had taken the edge off his nerves and the Duke was beginning to relax. As anxious as Duke had been to get away from his club, from the ghetto and from Los Angeles, the whiskey had served to soothe that anxiety and erase it from his memory.

Duke now laughed easily with Jim and Eddie-Bee, and Joe wondered as he watched the easygoing men if his fears concerning Johnny and Buddy and the Duke's sudden trip to Las Vegas had ever really been justified.

14

THE BLACK CADILLAC was parked on Compton Boulevard in front of the Paradise Room, waiting for the Duke's trip to the airport. The old Buick that cruised slowly by was not seen by anyone who would have recognized it. The only man, Jonah, who had seen the car was now nothing more than a plastic bagful of unidentifiable ashes and burnt marrow.

"He's in there," Johnny Washington said coldly. "That bastard is inside!"

"No doubt, Johnny," Buddy agreed as he turned the corner and parked the car on Manchester Boulevard. The traffic was light and at the moment there was no one on the streets.

"You about ready, my man?" Johnny asked.

Buddy smiled and pulled out his nunchaku. He tapped the end of the hardwood stick against the steering wheel. "Yeah, I'm ready, Johnny."

Johnny pulled out his magnum, opened the barrel and checked his load. Six bullets, only six chances to blow the man's brains out. Johnny snapped the barrel shut and put the gun inside his jacket, holding it tightly in his hand. "Leave the keys inside the car, Buddy. We got to make it to the airport fast."

"Okay..., I dig where you're comin' from, Johnny."

The two young black men sat in the old Buick for a moment longer. Johnny knew that, once they left the car, they would be committed to a road with no end in sight. If they left right now and drove back to the airport, they would both be in San Francisco within two hours, sitting in a comfortable hotel room with their girlfriends with enough money to live on for the next half a year.

It had crossed Johnny's mind, the idea of splitting right now and forgetting about the Duke. But that's as far as the thought had gone. Johnny knew himself better than that. He knew that he would never be able to live with himself as long as the Duke walked the streets of South Central Los Angeles.

"The bastard's got to die!" Johnny said aloud.

"Damn right, Johnny!" Buddy agreed, tapping his stick against the steering wheel with a building kind of intensity.

"We got to get him now, Buddy. No other fuckin' time but right now!"

Buddy looked at his friend. "Let's go, man. We don't want the bastard splitting on us."

The two young men climbed out of the car and stood on the empty sidewalk around the corner from the Paradise Room. The night was cool and the air was damp. The usual noise and commotion found on this street corner in Watts was not present this night. Occasionally a car drove by, but that was the only indication that any life existed here this night.

Slowly Johnny and Buddy walked to the corner of the building. Johnny peered around the corner. The black Caddy was still waiting in front. He nodded back to Buddy, and the two boys walked quickly toward the entrance to the Paradise Room.

On either side of the front door were large bushes. Buddy slid himself between the bush and the wall on the right side while Johnny took his position on the left. They would have direct access to Duke as he left the club, no more than five feet either way between the two young men who were waiting anxiously to kill him.

Inside the Paradise Room Duke put the bottle of Jack Daniels down on the table with a thump. "Okay, men, let's make it to the airport!"

Eddie-Bee and Jim slid out of the booth and started walking to the front door ahead of Duke and Joe. The men were mellow, each having had enough of the whiskey to relax and let their guard down.

The two front men passed through the velvet curtains and finally stepped out into the night air. They stood at the doorway for one moment, scanning the street carefully before allowing their man to expose himself to the elements.

Buddy crouched in the bushes, not allowing himself to breathe, holding his nunchaku with the tight intensity that preceded its use. The small, black-skinned bodyguard stood no more than two feet away from him with his shoulder and head at a sideways angle.

Buddy saw in his mind his nunchaku stick whirling through the air directly into the side of the body-guard's neck. He saw also in the same image the stricken man being thrown into the other, taller body-guard who stood next to him.

Johnny saw the intensity in Buddy's eyes as he peered around the legs of the bodyguard and into the bushes on the other side of the entrance. He prayed that Buddy would not move too soon.

But the image in Buddy's mind was strong, and the young man felt his muscles building, the tension in his body increase as he slowly raised the nunchaku up and over his head. A short, inhuman scream was the only warning the small bodyguard had that death was approaching.

The stick caught the bodyguard exactly where Buddy had envisioned. The sickening crunch of the man's bones snapping and shattering broke through the night silence. Eddie-Bee screamed out as he felt the hardwood stick cracking his shoulder and break-ing through his neck muscles.

"Goddamn!" Johnny screamed when he saw the stick flashing toward its victim. The force of the blow staggered Eddie-Bee and he crashed sideways into the taller bodyguard. The startled black man was hurled right into the bushes where Johnny lay waiting.

Buddy had no time to pull his sticks together before the explosion of Jim's magnum resounded through the streets. The bullet caught Buddy directly between the eyes, and as the young black was thrown backward, half of his skull was being thrown up against the wall of the Paradise Room.

Johnny was only inches from the bodyguard who was now lying on his back in the bushes. The teenage black raised his own magnum, put the barrel against Jim's skull, closed his eyes and pulled the trigger.

The man's skull shattered into a million pieces. Johnny could feel the pieces of skull, the oozing masses of brain matter and the sickeningly warm wetness of blood soaking his face and shoulders. The bodyguard slumped forward and lay face down in front of the door. His partner lay crumpled next to him.

Johnny leaned for a second against the wall. He knew that Buddy was dead, and he knew that Duke was somewhere inside the club. His mind was working furiously as he tried to decide what to do. Should he run? Or should he barge into the club firing his magnum?

Duke stood just inside the door to the club against the wall. The moment he had seen Eddie-Bee's neck and shoulders smashed by the nunchaku, he had thrown himself back inside and up against the wall. The two shots had come mini-seconds apart, and now three men lay dead just ten feet away. The man was real angry, and he was frightened.

He looked across the entrance opening to Joe, who had assumed the same position on the other side.

Both men knew that Johnny was somewhere outside the door. Duke considered coming out shooting but decided that it would be safer to send Joe out first. He nodded to his tall, black-skinned man, waving his pistol in the direction of the street.

Joe tightened, knowing that there was a good possibility that instant death awaited him outside the door. He also knew that Duke would be angry as hell if he didn't follow orders. There was no choice in Joe's mind. He was well trained.

The moment Joe started to make his move, Johnny made his decision. He had quickly determined that against the two men he had no chance. He knew how Duke worked, and he knew that the shootout would most likely come between himself and Joe. Both of them might die, Johnny reasoned, and that would leave the Duke alive. Johnny had decided to make a run for it and try again sometime in the future.

As Johnny bolted from the bushes and started running down the sidewalk toward the corner where the Buick waited, Joe came out of the doorway shooting wildly into the bushes where Johnny had been. The bullets rang out as they skipped off the cement walls.

Joe then stopped long enough to spot Johnny turning the corner at the end of the street. He raised his magnum quickly, fired with one hand and hit the sidewalk just behind Johnny's fleeing feet.

The keys were in the ignition. Johnny cranked the

engine furiously, pushed down hard on the accelerator and threw the car into first. The heavy machine lumbered forward and finally picked up enough speed to spin the rear of the car wildly.

The big, bald man stood at the corner watching the old Buick skidding wickedly down the street. He did not fire but ran toward the Cadillac. Duke was now standing at the door, holding his gun at the ready.

"C'mon, Duke, we'll get the bastard!" Joe yelled as he jumped into the driver's seat. Without hesitating, Duke jumped into the passenger's side. The doubt and the insecurity that had plagued Duke earlier had now left. He was beginning to feel the old excitement of the kill in his veins, and he knew his chances were good. Only ten minutes before, he had been running from the action. Now, however, he was going after it head-on. He wanted in on the kill.

Joe threw the Caddy into first, and the screeching and burning of the tires shattered the strange quiet that had settled on the bloodstained street. They turned the corner and headed down Manchester toward East L.A. Johnny's taillights were still in view as Joe pushed hard against the accelerator and went after the black teenager.

The blood was already beginning to dry on the sidewalk in front of the Paradise Room when Detectives Spence and Baker screeched to a halt. The two men jumped out of their car.

"Goddamn!" Spence cursed as he surveyed the three massively destroyed bodies sprawled on the concrete. He walked over to where Buddy lay and stared down at the nunchaku stick that the young black man still had gripped tightly in his hand. It was an eerie, grotesque sight because the better portion of Buddy's head was oozing against the wall, dripping down slowly into the bushes.

"Buddy?" Baker asked, coming up next to Spence.

"Yeah, got to be," Spence replied.

"I'll get on the horn, Jim," Baker said, returning to the car and calling for support and ambulances.

Detective Spence pulled out his snub-nose .32 and walked carefully between the velvet curtains and into the Paradise Room. Al the bartender was curled up on the floor behind the bar. He was shaking with fear.

"Okay, buddy!" Spence yelled when he saw the frightened figure. "Hands over your head and on your feet." Spence held his gun with two hands, pointing it directly at the trembling man's head.

Al stood up slowly, not wanting to do anything that might throw the large black gunman off balance. As far as the bartender was concerned, Spence was the victor in a shoot-out with his boss. He prayed that the man would not kill him, also.

"Okay, get over here!" Spence ordered, holding the gun on the man as he walked from behind the bar and out into the center of the room. "Where did they go?"

The truth dawned on Al. Suddenly, he was filled with relief. "You the cops!!!"

"That's right, mister. Where'd they go?"

"I don't know," Al began, "I heard two cars take off. I thought everyone was killed…, man…."

The sound of the approaching sirens told Al that he was in safe hands now. At least the police wouldn't murder him in cold blood, or so he hoped.

The Paradise Room was filled with uniformed cops. Their guns were drawn as they stalked through the abandoned club, searching out every room. But Al had been the only remaining tenant.

"Shit," Spence said to Baker as the two men lit up cigarettes outside on the sidewalk. Crowds had gathered now, and the night was filled with sullen black faces looking in at the gruesome orgy of death. The ambulances had arrived and the three black corpses were being wrapped and put on stretchers.

"I know, Jim. A minute, maybe two. That's all we missed it by!" Baker felt the same tension that he knew his partner was feeling. Somewhere in the vast expanse of Los Angeles, the two men they were after were stalking one another.

At that moment, a uniformed officer raced over to where Detectives Spence and Baker stood.

"Sir!" the officer began excitedly. "There's a report of gunfire over at the Santa Fe railroad yards!"

Revelation flashed through Detective Spence's mind like a sheet of white snow. "Goddamn! Tom, the Washington kid's goin' back; he's taking them into his own turf!" Spence turned back to the uniformed officer "Get all available units over there! Put it on red!!!"

Spence led the way through the crowd to their unmarked car. As he gunned the engine and started out toward the yards, he turned to his partner.

"Goddamn, Tom, we should've guessed it!"

The freight yards were dark, the huge boxcars looming like a city of shadows, neatly stacked one against the other. Johnny Washington crept between two long trains, keeping at least a hundred yards ahead of the two men who were stalking him.

When he had first pulled up outside the yards, the young black man had temporarily wondered why he had come to the yards. Then he had realized that it was his own game. He knew the cars, how to climb them, which ones would be accessible and which ones would be trouble. It wasn't much, he knew that, but at least it gave him a small edge over the two black figures.

As he had bolted out of his car, with the headlights of the Cadillac coming closer every second, Johnny had run to the fence and jumped it without concern for the barbed wire on the top. He had felt his skin tear as he hurled himself over and down into the yards.

Then he had heard the sound of the magnum firing, then felt the concussion of the explosion as it reverberated through the huge boxcars. The bullet had struck a car only a foot from where he stood. Quickly, before the next two rounds were fired, Johnny had thrown himself to the ground and had crawled beneath three cars, gotten to his feet and begun running through the darkened alleyways between the cars.

Duke and Joe had followed their prey over the fence and into the yards. Neither man had ever been inside the boxcar jungle, and they found themselves moving on pure instinct—Joe in the lead, Duke following close behind.

His heart beating wildly, Johnny had run as fast as his legs would carry him. He knew he had to put distance between himself and his hunters. Stopping for a moment, he listened to the approaching footsteps somewhere behind him. His mind racing furiously, he figured he had enough time to climb the ladder at the side of the car.

He grabbed the first rung and climbed the ladder quickly, throwing himself flat on his belly on the wooden top. The roof of the boxcar gave him a limited view down the dark alleyway between the trains. He held his magnum balanced against the edge of the roof and waited.

The two dark shadows stalking him appeared against the sides of the boxcars. Johnny held his breath, afraid that even his breathing would give his position away. The dark shadows moved closer.

Joe led the way. He was sliding tightly against the side of the cars, unwilling to expose himself at all. The footsteps they had been tracking had now ceased, and there was a dead silence throughout the area. Suddenly, Duke tapped Joe on the shoulder.

"You go up ahead. I think maybe he's tryin' to circle 'round behind," Duke whispered.

Joe nodded and began inching forward, his keen eyes searching frantically for some sign of the elusive black youth.

Johnny watched the tall black man approaching his car. It was perfect except for the fact that it wasn't

Duke. But Johnny would be satisfied with eliminating Joe. At least then it would be one against one.

Lowering the barrel of his magnum, Johnny held the gun tightly and sighted it at Joe's massive head. He took a deep breath, held it, then squeezed the trigger.

Joe's gun went off as the huge bullet shattered his skull, throwing him back against the boxcar. The two sudden flashes of light illuminated the entire area for a split second as though lightning had struck.

Johnny lay on the roof of the car holding his magnum with both hands and trying to keep himself from trembling. He knew that Duke was not far behind Joe, and he knew that Duke would attempt to run if he realized that his main man lay crumpled against the boxcar. He would have to make a move, and quickly.

At that moment, Duke had seen in the quick flash of light the body of his bodyguard flying through the air. He had heard the sickening crunch as the man hit the boxcar. Instantly, Duke had begun to back up, sliding against the cars in an attempt to get himself out of the yards.

Taking his shoes off, Johnny stood upright on the roof of the boxcar. He would take the chance and run Duke down. With light, noiseless steps, Johnny began creeping along the running boards atop the cars.

His movements were protected from the wary ears of Duke by the rumbling of a freight train pulling out of the yards. The empty tracks that the train was using were only yards away from where Johnny and Duke stood. Each man felt the ground begin to tremble as the huge train approached. And each man saw his means of escape in the approaching train.

The noise was becoming deafening now as Johnny leaped from one boxcar to the other without regard to the noise he was making. He looked over the tops of the other boxcars and could see the swirling lights of the engine as it approached them slowly.

Suddenly Johnny halted. On the ground, directly beneath the car on which he stood, he saw the shadowy figure of Duke. It was only a glimpse, but Johnny knew that he had his prey.

Duke moved along the base of the car, then reached the gap between that car and the next one. He started to climb across the huge metal links when instinct made him look up.

Johnny Washington stood with his legs spread, staring down at Duke from the roof of the boxcar. It had been a long time for Johnny, and the moment had finally come. But just firing the gun was too easy; there was too much involved. Johnny felt the need to linger for a second longer, just to capture for all time the look of death on Duke's face.

"This is for Leslie!!!" Johnny screamed above the roar of the freight train, which was now passing only two sets of tracks away.

Duke was trained and responded immediately to the figure of Johnny above him. He lifted his magnum and before taking aim, fired the gun repeatedly.

The first bullet struck Johnny Washington in the pit of the stomach, ripping through his intestines and

spewing blood and parts of his intestinal tubes out
through the gaping hole in his back.

As the white heat of pain shot through the young
black's brain, he fired his gun. But the force of Duke's
bullet had already staggered him, and he was firing
off balance. The bullet followed its aim and struck
Duke in the meaty portion of his left arm.

The young black man flew backward through the
air, hit the roof of the boxcar and rolled off, bounc-
ing once into the air as he hit the gravel. He was still
twitching as Duke stood above him and emptied his
gun into Johnny Washington's head.

Detectives Spence and Baker had to wait at the
crossing on Santa Fe Avenue for the freight train to
pull out of the yards. As the caboose crossed in front
of them, neither policeman noticed the crouching figure on the roof. Instead, they both cursed as they
crossed the tracks, heading toward the east side of the
yards.

A multitude of squad cars had already gathered near
the Buick and the Cadillac when Spence and Baker
pulled up. A young uniformed officer ran over to
them.

"There's a dead boy inside," the officer said.
"Name's Washington."

Detectives Spence and Baker walked through the
hole in the fence that the police had cut the moment
they arrived. The freight yards were now almost completely illuminated with spotlights and flares.
Uniformed cops stood guard against each boxcar as

the two detectives followed the young policeman through the maze of cars toward the dead youth's body.

Johnny Washington's body lay face up, his back twisted and broken by the fall. His face was only a pulp of bone and blood, and where his mouth had once been there was only a disgusting mass of flesh.

Detective Baker felt his stomach churn as he looked down at the mutilated body.

Jim Spence took the wallet from the officer who knelt down beside the body. He flipped it open and saw the photograph of the good-looking young Negro on the driver's license.

"Yeah," Spence said bitterly, "it's Washington."

The police officer looked up at Spence. "Looks like you got your killer, Detective."

"No, man," Spence replied coldly, "we got ourselves a young hoodlum. The killer's still out there somewhere!"

They searched the railroad yards through the long and chilly night, but the man known as Duke had vanished.

It wasn't until Detectives Spence and Baker sat over a cold and uneaten breakfast that the image of the passing freight train crossed their minds. Both men jumped, knowing that they had solved the mystery. But by that time, it was far too late.

Donald Goines
SPECIAL PREVIEW

ELDORADO RED

This excerpt from Eldorado Red will introduce you to Charles Williams, otherwise known as "Eldorado Red," who has been running a successful numbers operation in Detroit until his resentful young son moves in and interferes. It is again a realistic novel based on Donald Goines' own personal experiences. Eldorado Red is the vicious story of crooks who get richer with the dollars of the ghetto poor. Williams has it all—new cars, mellow women, and plenty of money—until one of his numbers pickup houses is robbed, and then a second. His men move only one step ahead of the cops as they try to discover who is behind the big grab.

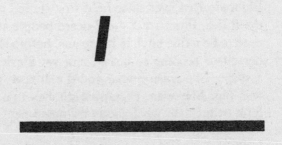

SHIRLEY BOOTH HANDLED the small compact car as if it was a toy. She drove like a man. Every now and then she'd glance at the younger woman sitting next to her.

"Dolores, do you think you'll ever learn this numbers route? It's so damn spread out, you know. That's the problem. Sometimes I wonder if it's even worth it, running all over the damn place picking up each customer's play."

"I've just about got it down pat now, Shirley," Dolores answered quickly. "It's just the small stops like the one we're going to now that get me mixed up. Too many damn small stops, if you ask me,"

Dolores stated sharply as she glanced over at the older woman.

As the women became silent Dolores wondered idly why Shirley had never become bigger in Eldorado's numbers outfit. She had been with Eldorado Red ever since he'd first started out back in the fifties. From what she'd heard people say, Shirley used to be a fine bitch in her prime, before she allowed herself to become so heavy, and yet Shirley still had a shape. She wasn't what you'd call real fat, but she was big. She wore expensive clothes that made her look better than what another woman her size would look like in cheaper clothes.

Shirley turned on the freeway and drove over to the west side. She came up on Grand Boulevard and made a right turn at Ford's Hospital. At the first side street she made another right. She parked in front of a dilapidated house that sat back from the street. It was a small house that had once been painted white, but now from neglect the paint was peeling and it looked as if no one had lived in it for years.

As the two women walked up the long pathway leading to the front door, they both noticed someone watching them from one of the front windows.

"Goddamn it!" Shirley exclaimed loudly. "This damn place really gives me the creeps. Every time I have to pick up here I hate it. I'll be damn glad to give this route to you."

Dolores gestured at the long weeds that had taken the place of the grass. "Well, it does look like a jungle out here, but I would think a lawnmower would take care of that little problem."

"Honey," Shirley began, "it's not the grass that I'm talking about. Wait until you get inside the house. It will make the outside look like heaven, plus the fact that you have to put up with both those old bitches inside. Shit, a nuthouse would be a better resting place for them than here."

Before she could knock on the front door, it opened. As they started to go inside, Dolores stated quietly, "You're too cold, Shirley. One day we'll...." The sight of the old woman standing behind the door stopped Dolores' flow of words. Dolores stared at the old woman in surprise. She looked as if she wasn't a day under one hundred. Her skin was wrinkled like nothing she'd ever seen before. But the real shock was the eyes staring out of the black face at her. There was a gleam in them that spoke of madness.

"Lordie, lordie, lordie," the woman shouted at them like a parrot, "come on in, come on in." She held the door only halfway open so that the women had to squeeze past her.

As Shirley entered, she wondered for the thousandth time why Eldorado Red continued to carry the women. It was true that when the two sisters' brother was alive it had been a good stop, but he had died over five years ago, and since then the place had fallen off until it really wasn't worth the trouble for the field worker to stop there. It was just too small. Sometimes the sisters didn't have fifty dollars for their day's take, but she knew if she had brought the matter up to Red he'd just say every little bit counts.

This was the first time Shirley had brought Dolores to this stop. She glanced out of the corner of her eye to see how the slim, brown-skinned young woman was taking it. It was really a change from the other homes they went to. There was a look of total surprise and fright on Dolores' face at the sight of the horde of roaches running wild on the walls of the front room.

"Where the hell is Auntie Dee?" Shirley asked sharply. She didn't want to stay in the house for any length of time if it could be avoided. The roaches didn't frighten Shirley, but she didn't like the thought of one of them falling on her. It made her flesh crawl.

"Auntie Dee is the one who picks up the numbers in the neighborhood," Shirley explained to Dolores. "She takes care of all the work. This poor thing here ain't too much help, she don't understand too much other than the Bible. She'll talk you to death about that, but nothing else."

"Have a seat, have a seat," the old woman yelled in a shrill voice, waving the women towards a dilapidated couch that was covered by a sheet and a blanket.

Before Shirley could warn her, Dolores started to sit down. A mouse ran from under the couch. Dolores screamed and jumped on top of the couch. There was no way Shirley could stop the flow of laughter that was taking control of her. She bent over and laughed until tears rolled down her face.

Dolores never took her eyes off the mouse. She watched the rodent go under the huge, old-fashioned china cabinet that stood against the wall.

"Little Jesus, little Jesus," the old woman scolded as she banged on the china cabinet. "You bad thing you, scaring the woman like that."

"Now, now, Auntie," Shirley interrupted, "that ain't necessary you takin' on like that. It was my fault for not telling Dolores that you kept a few pet mice and rats around."

At the mention of rats, Dolores' eyebrows shot up and she glanced around nervously. She started to say something but the sound of a harsh voice coming from behind a curtain leading into the kitchen stopped her.

"Ya'll have to keep that fuss down out there if you expect me to ever finish writin' up these here figures."

"Is that you, Auntie Dee?" Shirley asked, knowing all along it was the woman she was looking for.

"Of course it is, child. Who'd you expect it to be? Maybe Miss World or somebody like that?" the woman behind the curtain yelled sharply.

Before Shirley could stop her, Dolores was up and heading for the kitchen. Possibly because of her fear of rats, she didn't wait for Shirley to lead the way. Shirley followed the younger woman even though she had never gone any farther than the front room. Her curiosity was aroused.

The elderly woman sitting at the kitchen table looked up in surprise as the two women came barging in. But the person who was really surprised was Dolores as she stopped and stared open-mouthed at the old woman in front of her. She was utterly unlike any woman Dolores had ever seen. The impact of her presence was almost tactile in the silence that greeted their unwelcome entry. The old woman was as black as her sister. Neither woman had that rich night-shade velvety blackness that had its own sable beauty. Instead, the woman sitting in front of them had a gray-black shade with a deeply purple tinge about her lips. Her face was a mass of wrinkles that made her seem immensely old. But her eyes were the feature that held them. There was an evil glare in the pinpoint pupils—an undeniable quality of evil that could not be hidden.

"Well?" the old woman asked sharply in that husky voice that seemed to come from the emptiness of a deep well.

This was not the first time Shirley had met Auntie Dee. Ever since the death of her brother, Auntie Dee had been handling the numbers route, so Shirley was acquainted with the woman. But for some reason, the sight of Auntie Dee always gave Shirley a sense of fear. The old woman had never done anything to her, but the feeling was there just the same.

"Ya'll could have waited just as well in the front room for me to finish addin' up these here figures instead of running all over my house this-ways," Auntie Dee stated harshly.

Shirley had no doubt that the woman could see she was blushing. For something to do, Shirley fumbled around in her purse and found her eyeglasses.

"Sorry about this," Dolores spoke up loudly. "It's my fault we came barging in your kitchen. I heard your voice and just didn't think. We're running late today, so I just wasn't thinking."

"This goin' be my new pick-up girl?" Auntie Dee asked sharply, writing out numbers on a slip of paper.

"Yes, I'm the person who'll be stopping to pick up your stuff every day," Dolores replied. Suddenly she noticed something over the stove on the wall. It looked as if the wall was alive. It moved. She shook her head and squinted at the wall again, and again it seemed to move.

Auntie Dee finished writing out her figures, folded up the paper and stuck it in an envelope which held some other slips. "It seems as if my route's gettin' smaller every day," Auntie Dee offered as an excuse as she held out the envelope. "There ain't but twenty-eight dollars inside, but things goin' pick up. Ya just have a little patience with me." There was a slight hint of pleading in her voice. The few extra dollars they made off the numbers route probably helped the women pay off many of their bills.

Dolores didn't notice the envelope being offered to her. She was too busy trying to see what was on the back wall of the kitchen. Shirley reached over and took the envelope from Auntie Dee's hand.

After glancing at the figures on the outside of the package, Shirley shook her head. "I don't know, Auntie Dee, it's gettin' awful small. You had better try and pick up some of your old business. Why, we used to pick up as high as two hundred dollars a day through the week here. This kind of take," Shirley shook the envelope, "this ain't worth the price it cost us to pay Dolores here to come pick up."

"Ouch, Goddamn it!" Shirley cursed loudly as

Dolores backed up on her foot. "Watch what the hell you're doing."

Dolores didn't even hear her in her haste to get out of the kitchen. Shirley grabbed her arm and held her tightly. "What the hell's wrong with you?"

For a minute Dolores couldn't speak, she only pointed. "On the wall, over the stove. Is it what I think it is?" she finally managed to say.

As Shirley adjusted her glasses on her nose, Auntie Dee spoke up. "Shit!" she exclaimed loudly. "Where's that child been living? She ain't never seen a few roaches before?"

By now, Shirley could make out the black mass of caked up roaches. There were so many of them that it seemed as if the wall was alive. They seemed to move in unison. There were so many of them that you could take a piece of cardboard and scrape them off without reaching the wall underneath. Roaches living on top of roaches. The smaller ones on the bottom had been crushed to death by the larger ones on top. It seemed to Shirley that the wall held more roaches than all the roaches she had ever seen in her life. Putting together every roach-infested house she had ever been in, none of them had ever come close to showing such a display of filth.

The fear that Dolores felt only added fuel to Shirley's own terror. Ordinarily the sight of a few roaches wouldn't have disturbed either woman. But so many at one time was a terrifying sight.

"My God," Shirley murmured as she backed out of the kitchen with Dolores clutching her arms. And it was a good thing the women backed out, because over the doorway was another mass of roaches. As they tumbled through the doorway, the footsteps jarred a few of the roaches loose and they fell down on the women.

"Oh, ooooh shitttt! Goddamn it!" Dolores screamed as she brushed the roaches off her arm.

Shirley thought that the creatures had fallen in her hair. She reached up and snatched the expensive wig off her head. She shook it out as she fled from the house.

Auntie Dee followed the women out of the house and stopped on the porch. She stared after the running women in shock. "Why, I never," she began, then shook her head. She turned and glanced at her sister who stood in the doorway holding the envelope that Shirley had dropped.

"Can you believe grown women could act like that at the sight of a few roaches? I do declare, women ain't women no damn more." Then it dawned on her what her sister was holding. She grabbed the envelope out of her sister's hand and rushed down the narrow sidewalk as fast as her skinny legs would allow, waving the envelope.

"Hold up there, gal, you done run off and left everything," she screamed as she ran up to the car.

Shirley sat behind the steering wheel crying hysterical tears as she held her wig. Neither woman had gotten complete control of themselves yet. "My God," Shirley murmured softly, "the sight of them things made my flesh crawl. I still feel as if I've got the fuckin' things all over me."

Auntie Dee banged on the window. "Here, child, ya done run out and left the figures. I don't know what got into you girls, acting like that."

For a minute Dolores just stared at the woman peering in at them. She couldn't quite understand what Auntie Dee was saying. It was more her nerves than anything else that caused laughter to build up inside her. It was like a relief valve, releasing the tension that had been built up inside. Dolores laughed so hard that tears ran down her cheeks, while Auntie Dee stood outside the car banging on the window waving the policy slips wildly.

Shirley knew she should do something, but for the moment her brain locked on her. She couldn't get her thoughts together. The wild laughing of Dolores didn't help matters either. She started the motor so that she could let the window down and receive the package that Auntie Dee kept waving so crazily.

The sound of the motor starting put Auntie Dee in a frenzy. "Just a minute," Shirley yelled as she let the window down.

None of the women had noticed the police car that had pulled up beside them. They were all too occupied to pay any attention to what was going on outside. Shirley was reaching out for the envelope that contained the numbers when the policeman knocked on her window.

As Shirley glanced over her shoulder and saw the policeman knocking, the first thing that crossed her mind was that she was busted. There was no doubt about it. The policemen had heard Auntie Dee scream-ing about the numbers inside the envelope.

One quick glance at the policemen brought Dolores back to reality. She realized that she had a pocketbook full of numbers. The only thing she didn't realize was that they were already busted. She had no way of knowing that the officers had watched most of the proceedings. What they hadn't witnessed themselves they could just about fill in from the shouting Auntie Dee had been doing. There wasn't the slightest doubt in their minds as to what the envelope held.

Shirley tried to straighten up. She knew that they were on their way downtown and that there was no reason for her to look like a tramp. She began to put the wig back on.

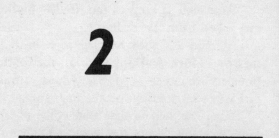

2

CHARLES WILLIAMS STOOD in the bathroom and admired his physique. "Not bad," he said as he patted his growing stomach. Charles stood over six foot two barefoot. His physique wasn't anything a young man in his teens or early twenties would have been proud of, but for a man forty years old, it was above average. His stomach was too fat, but other than that, he could justly say he was in good shape. He still possessed all of his teeth, bragging that he had never even had a toothache. He wore his hair cut close in a neat natural that was graying at the edges.

Charles stepped on the bathroom scale and the needle went up to two hundred and ten pounds. Charles

grinned as he got down and did ten quick pushups.
"Not bad," he said again, not in the least out of breath.
"For an old man, I'd say, Eldorado Red, you're in the
best of health."

"Were you talking to me, Red?" his latest young
girl asked from the bedroom.

Eldorado Red took one last look in the full-length
mirror before walking out of the bathroom. He
pranced around the bed. The young, attractive black
girl was stretched out on the lush spread.

"Tina," he said in that loud voice of his, "I'd say
you are about one of the luckiest bitches in this cold
old world we live in."

Tina tried to frown. "You know I don't like that
word, Red. I ain't nobody's bitch, and I don't like to
be called one either."

Red stopped his prancing and glanced down at her.
"Hey, baby, how many times do I have to tell you that
bitch is a term of endearment? It depends on what
tone of voice the person uses. Now, when I spoke of
it a minute ago, I was really only using it as a figure
of speech. If you found something depraved about the
word, honey, it's in your own little mind."

For a minute Tina just stared up at him, then she
sat up on the edge of the bed. "There you go again,
'Rado Red, using them words. When you start talking like that, you make everything seem right."

Charles Williams, better known by his friends as
Eldorado Red, just smiled a cold, bitter smile. It was
the smile of a man who had seen just about everything there is to see. "Tina, you are one lucky girl.

For one thing, you don't think too much. At least I don't believe you do anyway. All you're concerned about is a pretty dress and learning the latest dance steps."

The irony in his voice was missed by Tina. "You goin' let me go shopping today?" she asked greedily.

Just as quickly as his good mood had come, it vanished. Tina watched the tall, light-skinned man stride over to the dresser and pick up his pants. He slipped them on quickly, reached in the pocket and counted his money.

"Here, honey," he said as he peeled off a hundred dollars and tossed it on the bed. "When you finish shopping, rent you a room at a motel downtown somewhere. That way you'll be closer to the stores you like so well."

It took a second for Tina to realize it, but she had somehow managed to get on the wrong side of him. Eldorado was mad and she couldn't understand why. "Honey, you're not angry with me, are you?" she inquired sweetly.

"Angry! Why, baby, what could you possibly do to make me lose my cool?" he asked, smiling at her. Had she paid closer attention, she would have noticed that the smile didn't quite reach his eyes. They remained a misty gray—cold and bleak.

"Well then, daddy, ain't no sense me wasting no good money on no old motel room. Besides, I hate to sleep alone. I'll just do my shopping and catch a cab back here."

"No, I'm afraid you won't do that either," Eldorado

answered quietly. "When you leave, you'll take all the clothes you've been buying the past week with you." Before she could say anything, he went on. "I mean it, Tina, I don't like for a bitch to think she's playing on me. I've been kind to you all this week, honey, giving you money to go shopping, but I don't like for a bitch to try and hustle me." He waved her reply down. "Don't say it, it will only make matters worse, Tina. Yes, you did try and hustle me. Even if you don't have the sense to realize it, you did try. Every fuckin' day this week, I've given you better than a hundred dollars each day. As long as you didn't ask for it, it was all right, but today, honey, you let the cat out of the bag. So you take that little money and make the best of it."

She ran over to the man and put her arms around his waist. "Oh, daddy, I know it must be more than that to it. Did Buddy say something to you? 'Cause if he did, he was lying. I ain't had nothing to do with your son, even though he's been hittin' on me ever since I got here."

The coldness in his eyes became chilling as he stared down at the woman with her head on his chest. "Tina, I haven't even talked to my son, so don't say anything you might regret. If he's been hittin' on you, I don't want to know nothing about it."

Eldorado pushed the woman away from him. The thought that his son would stoop to hit on one of the chippies that he brought home filled him with a rage. He had been very good to the boy ever since Buddy had left his mother's home six months ago and moved in with him. He had tried to give Buddy everything a young boy of eighteen could want—his own car and clothes that any boy would be proud of. Anything Buddy wanted, all he had to do was ask for it. The very thought of his own son going behind his back after one of the cheap bitches that Eldorado brought home was almost unbearable. He didn't even want to look at the girl in front of him. Of course she was young enough to be his daughter, but that wasn't the point. He hated betrayal on any level. And the thought of his own son attempting to go behind his back was disgusting.

"Get out!" he ordered harshly. "Take your shit and get the fuck out of my sight, Tina. I mean it! I want you out of here as soon as goddamn possible!"

Tina took one look at his face and decided to follow his orders. He might change his mind and decide to take back the clothes he had bought for her. The thought of that happening filled her with more fear than the thought of a beating. She rushed around the room gathering up her stuff. Eldorado turned away from her and left the bedroom.

He walked out into his luxurious living room and sat down. Red reached over and tapped a switch on the couch and music came flowing out of the walls. The sound was everywhere. His glance went around his beautiful, eighty-thousand dollar home. It hadn't always been like this. It had taken hard work to get where he was. That was one reason why the thought of his son's betrayal hurt so much. He had been planning on teaching Buddy everything about his organization there was to know, so that one day he could just turn it all over to his only son. Eldorado Red laughed harshly. It wasn't a very pleasant sound coming from him. It carried the bitterness that he felt so deep down. Nothing had ever been given to him. He'd have been happy if his dad had given him a pair of shoes when he came up, let alone a new sports car and all the damn clothes a kid could want.

The years slipped past as he sat there and he remembered the cold days he had spent walking from house to house picking up each player's number personally and how he had had to turn in all the plays for over a dollar to another, bigger numbers outfit because his small bankroll couldn't stand a hit for over five hundred dollars. All the dime and two-bit plays were his meat at the time, but the day finally came when he could take the chance and hold onto some of the dollar bets. He'd been lucky then because nobody ever hit on him for over fifty cents.

What had made his name good was the way he paid off. Whenever someone did hit, whether it was for pennies, dimes or fifty cents, he'd personally make sure they got their money the first thing in the morning. As soon as he was sure the number wouldn't be changed, he'd be there with their money. His reputation for paying off quickly spread, so that soon new customers were asking for him.

Eldorado Red's numbers route grew from a small hundred-dollar-a-day route up to where he was picking up five hundred dollars a day. Then he had started hiring the girls to work for him. Shirley had been one of the first. He had given her his own personal route while he started to build up another one from the new customers coming in. It had been slow, but it had finally paid off.

Tina came out of the bedroom carrying her suitcase. "Eldorado, honey, I don't see why we should have to end up like this. I mean, we was getting along so fine, then all of a sudden we fall out. I don't really understand yet; what happened?"

Red just stared at her. "Did you call you a cab?"

When she said that she had, he added, "I think it would be best if you went out on the porch and waited on it, Tina."

Before she could say anything, they heard a horn blowing. "That's probably your cab now," Eldorado said coldly.

Tina gathered up her belongings. She started to say something to him, but his face was set in such hard lines that she changed her mind.

Red watched her walk out of his home and, he hoped, out of his life. He glanced at his watch. It was getting time to go over to his drop-off house and find out if everybody came in off their routes. He didn't anticipate any problems; he just received personal happiness from being around the receiving house when all the numbers came in. It filled him with pride to see all the money stacked up on the table. Red was a self-educated man so he took a lot of pride in his accomplishment. To know that he was the creator of his own organization, one that took in from five to ten thousand dollars every day, gave him much pleasure. Eldorado Red knew it wasn't what you would call a big outfit, but it was big enough.

Red walked to the window and watched the woman get in the cab. Good, that was one problem off his back. It would be a damn long time before he'd allow another bitch to move into his house, he told himself harshly. That was a mistake he could do without. Eldorado went back into the bedroom and finished dressing. Dressed in neat slacks and matching dark blue shirt, he checked the expensive watch on his arm to make sure he had enough time, then locked the front door behind him as he left. The bright red Eldorado Cadillac sat inside the garage. Eldorado had once taken pride in buying a new Cadillac every year. But now the cars were just another form of transportation.

That was the way life went, he rationalized. Things that you used to take pleasure in became common, unexciting and ordinary affairs. Maybe he was getting old; that could be one reason why nothing seemed like it used to be. At one time he would have never gotten mad at Tina, understanding that it was just a young girl's greed. Any black girl that had never had anything would have been carried away with what he had to offer. A beautiful home, a swimming pool in the backyard, and other things that he took for granted were exciting to a girl like Tina. But people like Buddy were different. Buddy took everything for granted, as if it were his due. Maybe that was the problem. He had never sat Buddy down and explained that no one owed Buddy or his mother anything.

Especially that bitch he called mother, Vera. A tall, brown-skinned woman who was too attractive for her own good. A woman who used her beauty for a tool to bend other people to her will.

Eldorado Red backed the long Cadillac out of the driveway. He didn't bother to glance back at the beautiful ranch-type home he was leaving. The well-kept lawn and the beautifully trimmed hedge that spoke of money were things that he had worked a lifetime to achieve. It didn't cross his mind that there was a possibility he might end up losing everything he had worked so hard to gain. But even at that moment, incidents were working that would push him to the wall. People were scheming to overthrow his small organization, and even as he drove slowly toward town, other people were riding, carrying guns. Their one motive was to relieve Eldorado Red of some of that hard cash they knew he had.

3

THE FOUR MEN RIDING in the car laughed and talked louder than was necessary. Wine bottles passed from the back to the front with frequency as they neared their destination.

"Goddamn, Buddy, you're sure now it ain't but five women and two men in this joint, man?" a fat, dark-complexioned young man asked for the tenth time.

Buddy, a tall, light-complexioned Negro, twisted around in his seat in the front of the car and glanced back at the man. "Listen, Tubby, my man, I ain't wasting my time settin' this shit up for nothing. When I say it ain't but so many people in one of these joints, I know what I'm talking about. If you're scared shit-

less, man, just say so. If you want out, it's damn near
too late for that. We done went over this shit for a
month gettin' the right people together and everything,
so now it's D-Day."

The men fell silent in the car while Tubby wiped
the sweat from his brow. He didn't want the rest of
the guys to know that he was frightened. Eldorado
Red wasn't no punk, no matter what Buddy said.
Tubby had been around for a long time and he knew
about a few of the things Eldorado Red had done when
he was climbing to the top of his field.

"Naw, man, I ain't scared; it's just that I'm thinkin'
close on this thing, man. It just seems as if it's too
easy. I mean, a guy like your old man just don't take
chances, Buddy. It's too pat," Tubby answered
doggedly.

Buddy gave him his practiced sneer. "My old man
is a punk, man. He don't know nothin' but how to
smell under some funky young bitch's dress. That's
all he's got on his mind, man, pussy. That's it, pussy,"
he repeated harshly as he thought about Tina and how
the fine young bitch had turned her back on him. How
the bitch could prefer his father to him, Buddy would
never understand. It hurt his pride.

Samson, a husky, brown-skinned brother, took his
eyes off the street for a moment to glance at Buddy.
"Your old man may be a lot of things, Buddy, but he
ain't no punk, man," Samson stated loudly. Whenever
he spoke the rest of the men paid attention because
Samson was the kind of man you respected. He wasn't
tall, but he was built wide, standing about five foot

nine with huge shoulders. His muscles seemed to move on their own when he walked.

"Yeah, man," Buddy replied coldly, "I done heard all that shit about how my old man handled the dagos when they tried moving in on his numbers outfit." He didn't try to conceal the contempt in his voice as he continued. "To listen to you guys tell it, my old man is one ball of fire. Yes siree, he's just too goddamn much."

The silence that invaded the car was heavy. Each man looked away from his neighbor as if he didn't want the man next to him to see the uneasiness that was all too apparent.

"Mother fuck-it," Samson stated coldly. "If you want to fool yourself, Buddy, that's all right with me, but don't think I'm buying that shit. Ain't no fools in this car, man, you can bet on that. Each and every one of us know just what we're gettin' into. Your old man might not do nothing to you about knockin' off one of his joints, but he'll bury one of our black asses if he ever gets wind of it being us who knocks off this pickup."

"Amen to that!" Danny, a slim, jet-black drug addict, stated. "It ain't no motherfuckin' doubt about it going any other way than that way, man. When we fuck over Eldorado's shit, the dues are going to be mean for whatever nigger gets his nuts caught in the sand. Me, I ain't worried 'cause I'm pullin' up for the Big Apple tonight, right after we split up the cash."

"You been going to the Big Apple ever since I met you, Danny," Buddy replied harshly. "The furthest you goin' get with your money, man, is the nearest dope house."

"Dig this, my man," Danny began, "if I don't never get to New York it ain't nobody's motherfuckin' concern but mine. Maybe I find my thing in talkin' about going to the Big Apple. But whether or not I go is still my business and not yours, my man. So don't be so quick in calling me a lie, 'cause you don't know me that well, man, and I really don't like for nobody to call me a lie."

The slim drug addict hadn't raised his voice, but the message was there loud and clear. Danny was a dangerous man, regardless of his size. Just how dangerous he was was well known by everybody except Buddy. Buddy was fairly new to the crowd. He had been with them long enough for them to have confidence in him. For the past three years, off and on, whenever Buddy came over for the summer to visit with Eldorado Red, he ended up running with the three men in the car. But Danny's friendship with Samson and Tubby dated back to their childhood days when they went to school together.

Something seemed to warn Buddy because he fell silent, letting the matter drop. But he didn't fear Danny. To him, Danny was just a dumb-ass drug addict, one he would squash if the small man ever got in his way. Instead of arguing, he let his mind wander. He thought about his mother and brother and sisters back in the cold-water flat in Chicago. Four women and one boy fifteen years old crowded together in one filthy four-room apartment. The very thought of it made his jaw tighten in anger. All that room that no one used at Eldorado's house, yet his brother and sisters and mother had to make use of a rat-infested building. He was the oldest of the children, and the only child his mother bore for Eldorado Red, but he still held his father guilty of his mother's problem. His mother had run out on Red when Buddy was only a year old, choosing a pimp with a new Cadillac and going to Chicago. One Christmas five years later she had called and given Red her address so that he could send some money for the child. After that, every month until the boy was grown, Eldorado Red had sent one hundred dollars to Chicago. If Buddy had asked, Red could have shown him money order stubs dating back fifteen years. But Buddy never asked; he enjoyed nourishing his hatred.

The sight of a police cruiser put all of the men inside the car on alert. Where before the men had been slumped over and relaxed, now they were tense. Nobody glanced over at the police car as they pulled up beside it.

"You goin' pass them?" Tubby asked excitedly as they drew up next to the policemen. Samson didn't bother to answer. As the policemen glanced over at the passing car, Samson pretended to be laughing then made a gesture with his hand as he talked. It was all play acting for the benefit of the policemen.

"What are the bastards doing now, huh?" Danny asked from the backseat.

"Just be cool, man, just be cool. The motherfuckin' pigs are still behind us, so just take it easy. I don't

think the cocksuckers have made up their cotton-
pickin' minds whether or not to fuck with us." It was
the same feeling that all black men had when they
saw the police. Whether or not they had done anything didn't make any difference. They were black and
that was enough. It meant it was open season on them.
At any time they could be stopped and made to get
out on the sidewalk with their hands in the air while
the car was searched.

This time they were dirty. There were three guns
in the car and that meant a prison term for each man
if the police decided to stop them and search the auto-
mobile.

"Man, if they look like they want to fuck with us,
let's make a run for it. Maybe if you can gain a block
on them," Danny stated in a matter-of-fact voice,
"we'll have time to throw these pistols out."

Samson glanced in his mirror. "They're stickin'
pretty damn close to our bumper, but if it looks like
they've decided to fuck with us, I'll do what I can.
Ain't no sense in layin' down like a wet duck."

"Bust a cap at them motherfuckers," Buddy said,
his voice shaking. "I don't want to go to no joint on
no bullshit. If we blast at their ass, maybe we can get
away."

"That's dead, baby. That's the coldest shit in town.
The last thing in the world we want is a gunfight with
the police." Samson looked sharply at Buddy. "Are
you out of your fuckin' mind? We ain't got no reason to hold court. Even if they stop us, everybody
ain't got to fall. So they find some fuckin' guns in the

car. They don't have to belong to everybody. I'll ride the beef out first before I'd let everybody fall on the same motherfuckin' charge."

Buddy wiped the sweat off his brow. "Okay, my man," he said with a smile. "Just remember your words. If we get uptight I hope you remember everything you just said." He hesitated for a second, then added, "I can dig where you're coming from, though. It don't take everybody to do one bit."

As Samson glanced at him sharply, Buddy continued. "As far as I'm concerned, I don't know nothing about no guns. All of them are still in the glove compartment, ain't they?"

Danny laughed bitterly. "You're one cold motherfucker, Buddy. I wouldn't trust you in a shithouse with a muzzle on."

"What the fuck do you mean by that?" Buddy asked quickly. "If you got something on your mind, man, come on out with it!"

Suddenly Samson let out a breath of relief. "The motherfuckers turned off. They must have got a call or something. I'd have bet a twenty-dollar bill against a bucket of shit that they were going to fuck with us. It just goes to show, you can't never tell."

The men relaxed and joked back and forth the rest of the way. It was as if the police car had taken all the tension out of the robbery. Now they were ready. Samson parked the car a few doors down from the apartment building they were to enter.

As they sat in the car waiting for the delivery man to arrive, Buddy scanned the street searching for that

Eldorado that he knew so well. He let out a sigh of
relief when he didn't see the car. If the other men
knew that there was a chance of Eldorado Red showing up, they'd call the job off. Buddy prayed under
his breath that this was one of the days that Red would
be late showing up or wouldn't bother to stop by.

The sudden appearance of a catering truck brought
the men up in their seats. "Is that the one that deliv-
ers the food?" Danny asked from the back.

"More than likely that's it," Buddy replied. "Like
I said, they use a different delivery service just about
every day. That way the drivers of the trucks don't
get any ideas."

"You better get ready, Danny," Samson ordered as
he reached over and opened up the glove compartment. He quickly removed the guns and passed them
out. "Buddy, you go with Tubby and bring back the
driver. After that, you can sit the rest of the caper out
just watching him."

For a brief second Buddy hesitated. He had hoped
that he wouldn't have any reason to put a gun in his
hand. That way, if something happened, he could
always play on the fact that he hadn't used a gun.
Now, if he followed Samson's order, he would be
involved no matter what happened. The delivery man
would never forget him, he was sure of that.

His mind worked overtime trying to come up with
an excuse, but he couldn't find one that was usable.
It wasn't that he was scared, but Buddy just didn't
want to get involved if it was possible for him not to.

"Well, my man, what the fuck are you going to do?

Let the man get away?" Samson asked sharply.

For an answer, Buddy opened up the car door and got out, followed closely by Tubby. The two men approached the driver of the truck quickly. "All right, mister, don't breathe too hard if you know what's good for you," Buddy said as he stuck the gun into the ribs of the truck driver.

The driver, a heavyset Negro, started to raise his hands. "Just take it easy, kid," he said. "I ain't got enough money on me to die for. You can have every fuckin' thing you see. This is just a job to me; I don't owe the company enough of anything to lose my life over."

"Just keep your hands down then," Tubby ordered from the other side of the man. "You don't give us no trouble and we won't give you none. Just follow directions like you got good sense, my man." Tubby's voice was low, but there was no mistaking the determination behind the orders.

"We don't want your money, man, we just want to deliver those dinners for you, that's all," Buddy stated, then added, "Now, I want you to walk with us back to that car down the street. Just act normal, you know, as if we were old friends."

SPECIAL PREVIEW SECTION FEATURE

Again, based on personal experience! When Donald Goines was discharged from the Air Force, he was addicted to heroin. To support his habit he staged the robbery of a local numbers house. And from that experience came *Eldorado Red*! It's the vicious story of crooks who get richer with the dollars of the ghetto poor. Charles Williams, otherwise known as Eldorado Red has it made— new cars, mellow women and plenty of money. Then he learns that treachery falls at the feet of his own son!

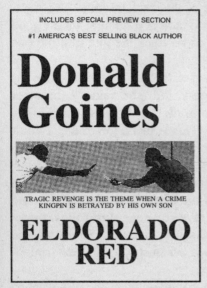

INCLUDES SPECIAL PREVIEW SECTION

#1 AMERICA'S BEST SELLING BLACK AUTHOR

Donald Goines

TRAGIC REVENGE IS THE THEME WHEN A CRIME KINGPIN IS BETRAYED BY HIS OWN SON

ELDORADO RED